CONRAD: FALLING FOR THE GRAVEKEEPER

CONRAD'S STORY

JANE LADLING MYSTERY SERIES
BOOK FIVE

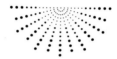

GENA SHOWALTER

JILL MONROE

Cover Created by Leni Kauffman

Editing by AZ Editing

Proofreading by Naomi Lane

Chapter Header by soleilc through Depositphotos.com

Ornamental Breaks by CRStocker through CreativeFabrica.com

This book is dedicated to our patrons. We are eternally grateful for your support.

Special thanks goes out to Naomi Lane—you're a rock star.

We could not have gotten through the year 2022 without our dear friends and families. Thank you.

CHAPTER ONE

Make sure your knock is authoritative, to the point and
certain. That way, people know who they're dealing with
before a word is ever spoken.
—A Gravekeeper's Guide to Dating

Special Agent Conrad Ryan remained behind the
wheel of his government issued sedan, parked in a
lot with three other vehicles. The same spot he'd occupied all
night. Morning sunlight framed the rat trap motel before
him. An Atlanta staple often touted as The Full Monty. It was
also the site of two upcoming arrests.

"If a suspect runs," Tim Barrow said from the passenger
seat, "you've got to do the chasing. It's your turn."

Conrad didn't spare his partner a glance. He continued to
scan the area, on the lookout for anything troubling. With a
tone drier than dirt, he replied, "Funny how it's always my
turn."

"Isn't it?" The other agent shifted in a failed attempt to get
more comfortable, then reached over to pat Conrad's shoul-

der. "But you really can't complain. You're young and in the prime of your life."

"What are you, forty? That makes you five years older than me."

"I'm thirty-nine, but I've got a wife, kids and a mortgage. You gotta add a decade for each. The stress, don't you know."

Please. Tim Barrow adored his family. Something Conrad didn't have and didn't want. He'd rather solve cases than spend time with people. Any people. Although, yes, his days had become pretty monotonous. Climb out of bed, guzzle coffee, investigate a murder while marveling at the depths criminals sank, jog five miles, try and fail to sleep. Repeat.

"What's wrong with these seats?" Barrow rubbed his lower back. "When will the warrant come in?"

"Any minute." As soon as they received the go-ahead, they'd make the apprehensions, close a case, and finally head home. Unless one of the suspects left the motel room, thereby endangering others. Then Conrad had a legal right to kick into action, warrant in hand or not.

"Distract me from my aches and pains." With a groan, Barrow shifted again. "Tell me how things went with Tonya last night."

Conrad swallowed a groan of his own. Why had he ever mentioned the date? Seriously? Why? Sharing personal information only invited further inquiries about his life. Even at his best, he wasn't exactly an open book. He possessed an inner circle of one—his foster brother Wyatt—and he had no interest in welcoming a second member.

"'Cause you know," the other man added, "Margot has set her sights on a second chance with you."

Oh yeah, that was why he'd mentioned the date. It had stopped a matchmaking attempt. Or so he'd hoped. Coworkers who played cupid were the worst.

"I'd rather not discuss Tonya and Margot." Tonya, the

CONRAD: FALLING FOR THE GRAVEKEEPER

beautiful accountant who'd treated a server like a servant, ensuring Conrad wanted nothing to do with her. And the perfectly pleasant Margot, a friend of Tim's wife who'd been a poor fit. For some reason, Conrad had failed to relax in her presence.

Actually, he failed to relax with anyone but Wyatt.

A ding sounded from Barrow's phone. He read the screen and whooped. "Guess who got that warrant?" He returned his gaze to the motel and frowned. "Perfect timing, too. The boyfriend is on the move."

Sure enough. A male in his early twenties with scruffy hair, a wife beater tank, and a devil tattoo on his forearm exited room 214. A pair of shades hid his eyes. Stains littered his wrinkled jeans. He puffed on a cigarette before dropping it and stomping on the butt.

Two days ago, a distraught mother had showed up at Georgia Bureau of Homicide headquarters, claiming someone was demanding five hundred thousand dollars in exchange for her daughter. If she refused to pay, the young woman would die. Just like her roommate.

Hadn't taken long to verify the college student's disappearance and the roommate's demise. But evidence hadn't pointed to an abduction. No, the truth proved much more sinister. The daughter had poisoned the roommate, panicked, and tried to cover up the crime with a staged kidnapping via her boyfriend. The two planned to use the ransom money to fund a fresh start in another country.

"If the daughter exits, she's all yours," Conrad said, emerging from the vehicle. Oppressive summer heat enveloped him, baking him inside his suit. A sensation he'd lamented but accepted. What else could he do? Hand on his weapon, he stalked toward the suspect. "Troy Billingsley, I'm Special Agent—"

Billingsley jolted and sprinted off. With a sigh, Conrad

gave chase. He dodged a series of crumbling speed bumps before tackling the thief to the pavement.

The guy didn't go down easy. He fought, elbowing Conrad in the sternum. Sharp pain exploded through him, and breath gushed from his lungs, but his grip on Billingsley never lessened.

A shadow fell over them. "And that's another reason it's always your turn. I could have a major head start, and you'd still beat me to the finish line." Barrow bent down and snapped the cuffs in place. "Troy Billingsley, you have the right to remain silent…"

An hour and forty minutes later, Conrad and Barrow sat in an interview room with the mother, breaking the news. Her daughter was safe, but in custody, where she would stay. The woman crumpled, no part of her ready to accept her only child's starring role in this nightmare of a case.

"If you need anything else, feel free to contact someone at GBH," Conrad intoned, itching to bolt. This much emotion gave him hives.

Barrow aimed an incredulous look in his direction before whipping out his wallet and pulling out a card. "This has my personal number," he told her, thrusting the paper into her hand and giving her fingers a reassuring squeeze. "Call me if you need anything. I'll help any way I can."

"Thank you, Tim." She offered him a watery smile. Her gaze darted to Conrad, and the smile faded. She nodded stiffly. "Agent Ryan." Head high, she made her escape.

Barrow tsked at him as soon as the door shut behind her. "You never even offered the poor woman your first name?"

So? It wasn't like he'd intended to build a lasting friendship with her. "Your point?"

His partner barked a laugh. "I'm just happy we got this wrapped up so quickly. With Hightower slated to be primary on the next case, I might get caught up on my paperwork for the first time in a decade. But probably not."

The all-nighters never bothered Conrad; he rarely slept, anyway. But the chance to work on Stella, his car, should have thrilled him. So why wasn't *he* happy?

AFTER A PREDICTABLY SLEEPLESS NIGHT, Conrad headed to GBH headquarters, ready to right another wrong. Any wrong. Though he lived only three miles away, traffic turned the ten-minute drive into a half-hour commute. Classic downtown Atlanta. At least the view was nice. Morning sunlight dawned over sleek modern architecture and older buildings steeped with charm. Tree clusters displayed streams of hanging moss, bringing in a hint of nature to the cityscape.

He parked in his assigned spot in the underground garage, stalked to security and flashed his badge. An elevator carried him to his floor and straight into the bullpen. A large space filled with desks unhindered by cubicles. Scribblings made with dry erase markers covered clear walls and show-cased link charts for ongoing cases. Several phones rang in tandem, blending with different discussions between employees. The scent of coffee overshadowed all others.

Men and women moved about at a fast clip. Closed offices belonging to senior agents lined the perimeter, and that's where he found Tim deep in conversation with fellow agent Karen Hightower and their boss, Maxine Randall. Terse expressions and body language abounded.

No celebrating yesterday's victory? Didn't take a detective to know something bad had happened.

He joined the threesome. Wasting no time, he commanded, "Tell me."

Hightower didn't spare him a glance. The sleek brunette kept her attention fixed on the boss. "If you're sure—"

"I am," Ms. Randall interrupted with a sharp undertone. Though she neared retirement, her strength could not be called into question. She'd risen in rank when few female agents had walked these halls, let alone specialized in homicide investigations.

Conrad welcomed her no-nonsense demeanor. She never cracked a joke and often sent the toughest of men scurrying to their desks with a simple lift of an imperious eyebrow.

To be honest, he more than appreciated his team leader. He admired her.

"You'll do whatever grunt work you're assigned," she informed Hightower.

Grunt work? Hightower was due to be primary. Had she ticked off the boss and earned a punishment?

"Grunt work," the agent muttered, a muscle jumping in her jaw. "Of course. Happy to do it." Hightower marched off, anything but thrilled, her heels clicking against the tiles.

Conrad wasn't offended by the lack of acknowledgement. From the beginning, the decorated agent had reminded him of himself. Guarded. Driven. Focused. Even somewhat detached from the rest of the world.

Ms. Randall leveled her razor-sharp gaze on him. "You're in charge, Conrad. Tim will fill you in on the way. Karen will be at your disposal."

Hands in his pockets, he nodded. "Thank you, ma'am." He never minded partnering up with Barrow, a workhorse who excelled at putting his nose to the grindstone and getting things done.

"We've got a bit of a drive. Let me grab a jacket." The other man jogged to his office, where he donned a GBH windbreaker to protect himself from Conrad's "arctic" air conditioner setting inside any and every vehicle, then joined him at the bay of elevators. "We should beat forensics, since they haven't yet mobilized."

They went quiet as they made their way to the parking garage. No need for any lingering journalists, witnesses or family members to overhear case details.

Barrow climbed behind the wheel of his SUV while Conrad strapped himself into the passenger seat. Soon they were soaring along the highway, and yes, the air conditioner blasted at full capacity.

"Ever heard of Aurelian Hills?" the other man asked, following the promptings of the GPS.

"I have not."

"It's roughly an hour north of us. A small gold rush town steeped in history. A body was found at a local cemetery. The Garden of Memories."

Wait. He blinked. "A body...at a cemetery?" This required an investigation?

"The place is landlocked, with no new burials for years. Apparently, someone dug up a grave, opened the coffin and dropped in our vic. A thirty to forty-something male. The onsite groundskeeper claims she found him while doing morning rounds. Sheriff is at the scene and says the guy has a pretty fresh head wound."

"Possible accident?" An attempted grave robbing gone wrong?

"Not likely. The sheriff also mentioned a cleanup job. There are no footprints coming or going other than the groundskeeper's."

So. Someone, or multiple someones, committed the murder and, what? Tried to hide the body in a coffin, only to be interrupted and scared away before finishing the job?

Think this through. The groundskeeper wasn't a probable

culprit. She would've had time and opportunity to clean up the site with no one the wiser. Unless she endeavored to play cat and mouse games with authorities like the last perpetrator. Always a possibility.

Honestly, nothing surprised him anymore.

For the rest of the drive, Barrow chatted about his family. How he'd driven to this soccer game and attended that dance recital. Conrad made the appropriate noises to indicate he was listening. When you lost your parents and a younger sibling at the age of ten, spent a couple years bouncing from foster home to foster home, then all but rotted inside a center for troubled youths knowing no one was coming to your rescue, family ceased to be a source of solace.

His chest clenched. Without thought, he traced his fingers over the tattoos that extended past the cuff of his dress shirt. Images his little brother Corbin had drawn just before his death. Stick figures depicting their family of four. An almost unrecognizable representation of their lab, Burp–the name Conrad and Corbin had chosen, thinking they were hilarious. A rainbow because they'd just heard the story of Noah's ark in Sunday school.

The clenching worsened. *Focus.* Conrad shook the tension from his hands and worked to center his mind. Somewhere in Aurelian Hills, people waited to learn how and why a loved one had died. He couldn't bring back the dead, but he could help them seek justice.

"...so there I was, driving to bakery after bakery to find the quote unquote perfect unicorn cupcakes," Barrow continued, and Conrad realized he'd lost track of the conversation. "I truly thought–"

"In five hundred feet, turn left," the GPS interjected.

As the agent started up again, they passed a welcome sign. *Stay and seek your fortune.*

Conrad scanned the area. Typical small town, with a main

street, city square and multiple antique shops. Picturesque and quaint. The kind of place that could have come from an airbrushed photograph.

Barrow chuckled. "They take their gold seriously. Look at those names. The Gilded Scissor. The Treasure Room. Yellow Brick Abode Library. Gold Rush Museum. Maybe I should bring the kids here for a tour."

Poor kids. Conrad considered any organized event an unnecessary torture. No thank you.

Barrow missed a turn along the back country roads, but GPS rerouted. Soon they approached a stretch of land filled with an array of pine, wisteria and magnolia trees, fenced in by both stone walls and overgrown hedgerows. From a sea of businesses, car lots and residences to this. An oasis.

"You have arrived at your destination," the GPS announced.

This was a cemetery? A massive wrought-iron gate loomed before them, agape. Conrad examined the landscape with murder in mind as Barrow followed a winding gravel path at a snail's pace, passing colorful flower bushes, crypts and a small rock bridge. Where were the—ah. There. The headstones. They peppered the hills and somehow added to the beauty of the surroundings.

"This place is massive," he said. Lush green grass stretched for miles.

"File says seventy-five acres. The caretaker's cottage is at the northeast edge of the property." His partner shuddered. "Can you imagine it? Living out here among the dead?"

Conrad arched a brow. "You work with the dead every day."

"Yes, but I don't take the corpses home with me," the guy said, approaching a small, quirky cottage with ivy climbing over the walls. Rocking chairs decorated a wraparound porch.

GENA SHOWALTER & JILL MONROE

Barrow parked under the shade of a giant oak, next to the sheriff's cruiser and a hearse. No one waited nearby.

"Do you know the location of the burial site?" Conrad asked, scanning a maze of cobblestone pathways without signs.

"Only that it's plot number thirty-nine."

Which could be in any direction. "All right. Have a look around the immediate area, and I'll see if the groundskeeper is inside."

They emerged into the hot summer day.

Barrow wrinkled his nose. "What is that smell?"

Conrad breathed deep. The thick fragrance of magnolia and gardenias saturated the air, more than making up for the excruciating heat. "Paradise," he muttered.

As a gentle breeze rolled past, rattling limbs and leaves, cheerful chirps and trills reached his ears. He almost grinned. Maybe living among the dead wouldn't be so bad.

He ascended the steps, ancient wood creaking beneath his loafers. In the corner, an old-fashioned two-person swing swayed with his motions. Nearby, a hummingbird visited a bright red feeder that hung from an awning.

He raised a fist to knock on the front door and spotted a black cat sitting gargoyle-style in the window. Framed by lacy curtains, the feline watched him intently. For some reason, Conrad felt as if his murder was being plotted in three hundred and sixty-five different ways. One for every day of the year.

Focus. He rapped his knuckles against the wood. Once. Twice.

"Hi. Hello," a sweeter than sugar voice called. "You're looking for me."

He turned and found a slender brunette in a purple dress hurrying toward them and waving. Her gaze skipped over Barrow, landed on Conrad, moved away and return in a snap. She halted abruptly and looked him over from top to bottom, her expression softening. When she licked her lips, his jaw almost dropped. Was she...*leering* at him?

He double-blinked. She *was*.

Conrad nearly barked out a laugh. Never in the whole of his existence had a woman ogled him so blatantly or suggestively. Especially after using such a polite southern drawl. Just how was he supposed to respond?

He logged her details. Probably mid-twenties. Long dark hair and thick bangs bordered a delicate face boasting a fan of black lashes, pink cheeks, and red lips. A pretty package. Very pretty. Altogether, she reminded him of a frosted cupcake. The kind with sprinkles.

Surely this little slice of sweetness wasn't the groundskeeper.

As if she sensed the direction of his thoughts, she met his gaze–*punch*. The air evaporated from his lungs, and tension abandoned him in a rush. In that moment, he thought he might be peering at tranquility itself. Peace oozed from her big, blue irises and washed over him.

His brow furrowed. He must be having a heat stroke. He'd never reacted to another person like this. What's more, no one could put others at ease with a simple glance.

Could they?

Her attention shifted to somewhere over his shoulder, a range of emotions crossing over her features. From irritation to disgust, sadness, and anger. Lost in her thoughts after eating him up?

The corners of his mouth twitched. What was she even pondering? "Ma'am?" he prompted.

Lips forming a small O, she snapped into awareness. Lasering her concentration on Barrow rather than Conrad, she thrust out her hand. "I'm Jane Ladling. The owner and operator of Garden of Memories, where your loved ones rest in beauty as well as peace." She winced, growing flustered. "Sorry. Habit."

The company slogan? Why was Conrad fighting another laugh?

"No worries. I'm Special Agent Tim Barrow." The seasoned agent managed to blank his features, revealing nothing of his own thoughts. Something they'd learned to do for the good of a case. "We're told you found a body."

"Yes." She raised her hand, as if they were doing roll call in grade school. "That's me. Her. I'm the finder."

He detected no upset of any kind in her tone. Had living among the dead made her callous against the consequences of mortality?

Conrad strode down the porch, a bit too eager to close the distance. When those baby blues hit him a second time, he would swear the rest of the world vanished into the ether. Just for a second. But a second was far too long for his liking.

And was she sniffing the air in his direction?

Yes. Yes, she was.

Her cheeks flushed a deeper red. He *must* know what thoughts danced in this cupcake's head.

"Ma'am," he prompted once again. Bemused, he extended his arm. Up close, he noted the collection of freckles on the bridge of her nose. Freckles. A new favorite feature. Could she be any lovelier?

She shook his hand, unable to mask her trembles. "I'm Jane Ladling," she repeated. "This is my place." Goose bumps spread over her sun-kissed skin, and she forced a cough he didn't buy for a second. "The cat is Rolex, in case you were wondering. He's the employee of the month."

"Rolex?" Without thought, Conrad traced his fingertips over his wristwatch. A Rolex. Once his father's most prized possession.

"Because he's the world's best watch cat," she explained.

"And don't bother trying to win him over. He's never going to like you. Not that you want to develop a relationship with my cat." Looking flustered again, she wrung her hands. "You want to see the dead body, I'm sure. I mean, I'm guessing he's dead. The sheriff didn't verify my observation, and I didn't check for a pulse."

Did Conrad make her nervous? Why did the idea intrigue him? "I'm Special Agent Ryan. I have a few questions for you."

She mouthed his name, as if searing it in her memory bank. "So, um, nice to meet you. I mean, not nice, since someone died and all. But, um, yes. Also nice. Because you're a great person. Or I'm guessing you're great. I don't really know you. You might kick puppies in your spare time."

She cannot be real. His head tilted to the side, and he deepened his study of her. *Only gets prettier.* "You mentioned being the one to find the victim."

"Mmm hmm. I was making my morning rounds, planning my chores for the day, when I came across a disturbed plot." She motioned toward a cobblestone path. "Sheriff Moore is there now. Why don't I answer your questions along the way?" Not waiting for his response, she scurried off.

He slid a pointed what-just-happened glance to Barrow, whose serious demeanor finally broke. As the other man chuckled, Conrad started forward. He quickly caught up with Miss Ladling. The other agent followed but hung back, remaining a few steps behind.

Let the investigation begin.

CHAPTER TWO

Always smell amazing. If you exude the fragrance of dry
cedar and rich spices, even better. You'll make a certain
someone forget every thought in her head.
  –A Gravekeeper's Guide to Dating

"*Y*ou mentioned you own the cemetery." Conrad
maintained a leisurely pace beside the
enchanting Jane Ladling, cataloging the
immense sprawl of land knitted together by those winding
cobblestone walkways.

Wax myrtles stood in straight lines, delineating different
sections. Stone benches dotted soft rolling hills. The place
was more than paradise. It was heaven on earth.

"I did and I do, yes." Pride flashed over Miss Ladling's
lovely face. With her hands clasped behind her back, she
seemed to glide over the cobblestones. "An honor passed
down from generation to generation. Well, until me. I'm the
last of the Aurelian Hills Ladlings. Upon my dramatic but
lonely demise, our reign over the afterlife will end."

The sheer earnestness of her expression invited him to

agree with such an unshakable truth, and it was ridiculously charming.

Charming now? On top of enchanting? He pursed his lips. "Lonely demise? You plan to die alone?"

Her fingers fluttered to the base of her throat in a graceful ballet of movement. "I do indeed. I'm never falling in love, getting married or having children."

A thousand questions filled his head. No love, wedding, or kids...but was she single?

Focus on the dead body, not the brunette. "Good to know. Has anything unusual happened on the grounds recently?"

"No. And I would have noticed. Rolex and I roam the Garden twice a day, every day."

Doing what, exactly, since she didn't accept new residents? "No one you've come into contact with acted out of character?" Up ahead, a squirrel jumped from tree limb to tree limb.

"Nope. The guests were as calm and quiet as usual." Just as earnest as before, she told him, "Hardly anyone complained about anything."

He folded his lips under his teeth to silence a snort. "Have any *visitors* acted out of character?"

"Oh. Well. I'm not sure about them, to be honest. Years ago, I instituted a company policy. No interacting with strangers unless you want to, and I rarely want to. I value the truth, you see, and people lie far too often. The dead have nothing to give but honesty."

That, he agreed with. "When we're done at the site, I'd like a copy of your security feed." He intended to watch the footage himself. Every second of it. Probably in slow motion.

She cringed. "Yes. About that. I absolutely one hundred percent will give you all the security feed I have. Which are my handwritten notes. A to-do list, really. I wrote it as I made my rounds."

You've got to be kidding me. "You have no cameras?" He caught sight of someone near a mound of fresh dirt. An older fellow in uniform with a bald head and a full silver beard. The sheriff. Currently, he stared at the hole in the ground while wiping sweat from his brow.

They'd reached the crime scene already? A twinge of regret prodded Conrad. He should have walked slower.

"In my defense," Miss Ladling said, "I live in a small town. I really only deal with trespassers in October, so there's not a reason to pay for..."

Her words trailed off as he swooped around, becoming an obstacle in her path. He planned to castigate her for the lack of protection. But was it really his place? Better to excuse her now.

He removed his sunglasses. A move he usually executed to let someone know he meant business. This time, however, he wanted nothing to filter his vision of this woman. Because...just because.

Big mistake. Huge. The sunlight paid her absolute tribute.

When her lips parted with a sudden hitch of breath, he figured he'd intimidated her and sighed. He donned his most practiced smile, hoping to put her at ease and dampen his intensity. "Thank you for the escort. I need to examine the site without you. Please return to the house with Special Agent Barrow."

The other agent moved to her side. "Ma'am."

Disappointment flashed in her expressive blue eyes.

Why disappointment? No. Nope. Not a mystery Conrad needed to solve right now. The dead man deserved his full attention. If this cupcake was a killer, he would eat his shoes.

After sliding his sunglasses back in place, he pivoted and strode off, joining the sheriff, forcing all distractions from his mind. A little more difficult to do than usual, but in the end, he succeeded.

As he performed a preliminary examination of the area, other GBH employees began arriving in groups. Soon the cemetery buzzed with activity. Agents cordoned off the scene with yellow taps. Others placed evidence markers here and there, and a photographer snapped photos of the grave, body and surroundings.

A brief discussion with the coroner confirmed his suspicions. Yes, this was a homicide. Time of death occurred between the hours of midnight and four.

Baking in the afternoon heat, Conrad removed his jacket, rolled up his shirt sleeves, and placed his watch in his pocket. He jotted down information as it came. Victim was a local physician named Marcus Leon Hotchkins. Married to Tiffany Angelina Hotchkins. Thirty-eight years old. Six feet one. Blond hair, brown eyes. A jagged scar decorated his right hand.

No sign of his vehicle near the cemetery. Either he'd walked here, or someone had driven him.

After instructing the sheriff to find the victim's wife, Conrad returned to the cottage for a final chat with the groundskeeper, using a map he'd taken from another agent. Anticipation hit him as soon as the home came into view. He spotted a new vehicle in the mix of cars—a shiny red convertible. Who had paid her a visit?

His gaze zoomed to Miss Ladling, who waited on the porch, perched on a rocking chair next to a petite black woman who looked to be anywhere from forty to sixty. The other woman wore a vivid pink blouse and a huge necklace made of undetermined stones. The cat still hovered in the window, staring into Conrad's soul.

Miss Ladling shifted in her seat, her attention dropping to his tattooed forearms. Her eyes widened. Surprised by the ink? Nervous again? Both? Whatever the reason, she continued to exude peace.

He couldn't make sense of the contradiction but flashed another I'm-one-of-the-good-guys smile. "Miss Ladling, I'd like a word."

Wringing her hands together, she asked, "Do I need a lawyer?"

"I don't know," he said on his way up the porch steps, hating the worry etched in her expression. "Do you?"

She reacted as he'd hoped, rallying her confidence. "I didn't do the crime, so I shouldn't do the time. Right? Unless there isn't a crime?" Hope radiated from her expressive features. "Did Dr. Hotchkins trip and fall or something?"

Whoa. Perhaps Conrad needed to grab a fork and knife and get started on a loafer. "How did you identify the victim if you couldn't see his face?" he demanded more sharply than he'd intended.

A flash of chagrin. "We—*I* put two and two together. Think about it. Curly blond hair on the corpse. Missing doctor with curly blond hair. There's only one fair-haired doctor people can't currently find."

Right. "Small towns have the biggest mouths," he grumbled. The citizens tended to stick together too, keeping each other's secrets. "We'll be taking both bodies as well as the casket."

"Have you already dusted for fingerprints? Never mind. You can't say. I get it." Her tone veered between helpful and curious. "Before you ask, I've never spoken to Dr. Hots. Hotchkins," she corrected in a rush, blushing. "I mean, I spotted him a few times when I visited Dr. Garcia. And I know his wife. But other than that, I have zero connection to him."

"Good to know." That blush... He withdrew his notebook and wrote: *Ask gravekeeper out when appropriate.* "We're packing up to leave, but I'd like to discuss something with you before I go."

Movement drew his gaze to her companion. Oh, yes. The other woman, listening intently and one hundred percent unabashed. She lacked only a bowl of popcorn.

He offered his hand and his name. "If you'll excuse us for a moment, I'd appreciate it."

Miss Ladling apologized for a lack of manners, then introduced him to the newcomer. "Special Agent Ryan, this is Fiona Lawrence, my best friend."

Best friends, despite the age difference? Interesting.

The older woman examined him with schemes glinting in her dark eyes. "Are you single, young man? I see no wedding ring. Perhaps you have a significant other?"

An attempt at matchmaking right off the bat? He wasn't surprised. Similar questions had been asked during past cases. For once, he harbored interest but could do nothing about it. Yet. At least he now knew Miss Jane Ladling was single.

"Were you at the house this morning, ma'am?" he asked, redirecting the focus of the conversation.

"I wasn't. But why don't we get out of this heat, and I'll tell you what I *was* doing. I'll even whip up a batch of my famous blueberry pancakes. At some point, I might explain the impoliteness of ignoring an old woman's question. Although I've already deduced the answer. You are *very* single."

A lesson in etiquette and an insult all rolled together. Nice. "What makes you think so?"

Her gaze darted between him and Miss Ladling. "The eyes. The eyes always give you away."

Noticed his interest in the beautiful overseer, had she? "Thank you for the tip." He'd be more careful from now on.

He glanced at Miss Ladling, curious to learn her reaction to her friend's revelation.

She implored him with her gaze. "Yes," she blurted out.

"He wants those pancakes." Looking as if she were on the verge of whimpering, she smashed her palms together and waved them in front of his face. "Please say yes."

He thought he might regret this, but he said, "I'm sorry, but I don't have time. There are too many other places I need to be today."

From beseeching to disgusted in an instant. "You fool," she griped, nearly surprising another bark of laughter out of him.

Yeah, the regret was already parking a moving van in his mind. What was so special about blueberry pancakes?

Miss Ladling quickly righted her expression, displaying only polite disinterest, as if he'd somehow failed her and she had no more use for him. How was even *that* charming? "You mentioned you wanted to discuss something with me?" she prompted.

"Yes. I'd like a list of names. Everyone buried in Autumn Grove. And any of their visitors for the past month." In the pad, he wrote and underlined, *Learn how to make blueberry pancakes. No, a different breakfast treat. Something better.*

Blink-blink. "Have you been to a cemetery lately? We open the gates and people come in. I give directions if someone has trouble finding their loved one, but that's about it for public interaction."

First no cameras, then this. She'd admitted to not speaking to visitors, but he'd expected a bit of spying on her part. "People can wander around unsupervised, in any area, at any given time?" Maybe he'd witnessed too many senseless acts, but the thought of this cupcake living in such a remote location, unaware of those trekking around her space didn't thrill him. Did she keep records of who had purchased the plots at least?

"Well, yes. Kind of. Folks visit their loved ones to reflect on the past when the urge strikes, time allows or any other number of reasons. This is a cemetery after all, not a bank ripe for a heist."

She had a point. Still. He made a notation next to his last note–*Check local crime statistics*–and flashed another practiced smile. "I'll take any records you have."

"Yes, of course. I've already pulled the file. We're happy to hand over a copy, along with anything else you need. Or want." Twin pink circles suddenly painted her cheeks.

Another blush? Had the cupcake's mind gone somewhere it shouldn't?

Do not smile.

He frowned instead. Unrelenting amusement during a case? Who even was he right now?

"I'll make the copy," the older woman offered, easing to her feet. "You stay here chatting with the nice agent, hon. It's perfectly proper since you're both very single. Isn't that right, Special Agent Ryan? Did I guess correctly, or do I need to stay and chaperone?"

Had to admire her persistence. "No chaperone needed, ma'am."

"Well now. See how easy it is to be polite?" The older woman winked and sashayed into the house.

Conrad scrubbed away any lingering good humor before refocusing on Miss Ladling, whose cheeks burned an even brighter shade of pink. "Are there any unmarked entry points into Autumn Grove?" he asked.

"There are, but I kind of need to *show you* show you. Which I'm happy to do. Just let me grab a hat. I'll be right back." She darted into the house, calling, "Don't leave without me."

He stuffed his hands in his pockets and rocked back on his heels. She took the peace with her. Thankfully she exited only two minutes later wearing a monstrosity of a sunhat with purple stripes to match her dress. A monstrosity, yes. And yet...

"Nice, um, hat." Strangely enough, he meant those words with every fiber of his being.

"Thank you," she replied with pride. Down the steps she bounded, leading him from the cottage. "This way."

In a blink, she shifted into tour guide mode, sharing different facts about the cemetery. Her features softened when she spoke of a private area reserved for her family, something she clearly valued as much as honesty. With such a strong attachment to her loved ones, he could guess the kind of childhood she'd had. As idealistic as the one he'd enjoyed, before a senseless accident took away everything he treasured.

He tensed. *Inward shake.* "How large is the property?" Wait. He already knew the answer.

"We're up to seventy-five acres now. Over time, different Ladlings added to the grounds."

"That's a lot of land for one person to tend." Did she have any spare time? "Do you employee other staff?"

"There's no need," she assured him, explaining how the cemetery was full, and ending with, "New burials are done at —" the glaze of disgust returned to her eyes—"Aurelian Hills Cemetery on the other side of town."

He nearly snickered. "Not a fan of Aurelian Hills Cemetery, are we?" As they turned a corner, entering a circular clearing nicely shaded by a canopy of leaves, he forced himself to steer the conversation back to the crime scene. "Do you receive many visitors out here?" Her personally, not the cemetery. He'd grown a bit curious about, say, any frequently seen males. She might be single, but surely the men of her town approached her in droves.

"Someone comes out, oh, roughly once a week. Maybe twice," she said, misunderstanding his meaning. Clearly she assumed his question concerned the residents. He couldn't correct her without revealing his interest in her personal life. "I also give a midnight tour of the grounds once a month, though attendance is sparse."

New information. "Midnight tours, but no cameras." Did she have a total disregard for her own safety? "What security measures *do* you have in place?"

"Well, I have the gate up front and a brick wall around the acreage. Before you ask, I open the gate at sunup and close it at sundown. The hours depend on the season," she added as they turned another corner.

"You close it?" He'd seen no wires to indicate a remote could be used. "Manually?" At night? Alone in the dark? Oh yes, a total disregard. "Why?"

"Tradition?" The answer emerged as a question. "My grandmother would never forgive me if I installed an electric gate."

A live-in grandmother? Might be how she'd met Ms. Lawrence. "Is she retired?"

Utter heartbreak turned her big baby blues into open wounds. A brief flash, and yet far too long. "No, she passed away three years ago. That's when I officially took over."

"I'm sorry for your loss." He meant that.

"Thank you. I miss her so much, but at least I get to visit her often. We just had tea last week, in fact. Anyway, I was raised here. I know the land and its residents better than I know the townspeople."

Sympathy welled. "I get it. Trees and monuments never let you down, and the dead never leave." He felt that way about his car. She was always there when he needed her. Unfortunately, the living left you far too soon, whether wittingly or unwittingly.

Miss Ladling cast him a glance of understanding, and it

discomforted him almost as much as his uncharacteristic admission.

He cleared his throat and pointed to a smaller, crumbling version of her home. "What's that building?"

"That's the official business center, such as it is, and what I wanted to show you. I removed it from the map because I'm never in it. But the original cobblestone path to Autumn Grove begins at the back porch. At night, this is the easiest track to follow, with the fewest twists, turns and skunks."

He made another note: *Buy skunk repellent.*

Following more questions about the building, he pivoted in front of her a second time. Her eyes grew wide, and she babbled, "Yes? May I help you? Is there something else on your mind, Agent?"

"Please, call me Conrad." The words shocked him. But take them back? No.

She blushed again. "I'm Jane. I mean, you already know my name. But feel free to use it. Everyone else does. A few times, I've been called Jay Bird."

He enjoyed those blushes. And her rambling. He thought he might enjoy her, period. "Sheriff Moore mentioned you live out here alone." Conrad had asked the guy for details about her. For the case.

"I'm not technically alone. I have Rolex."

"And he's terrifying, but he's not a genuine form of protection." Conrad rubbed the back of his neck, determination to fix her security issues growing. Something needed to be done. Fast. "I'd feel better knowing you had more security. Or *some* protection, at the very least."

"I'll look into hiring someone, I promise."

Something in her tone left him questioning her commitment to follow through.

When she side-stepped, intending to go around him and lead the way, he moved with her. "I'm sorry, Jane, but I'd like to view the property alone." He pulled a business card from his pocket. The one with his personal number added in ink. He'd carried the thing for years, never willing to part with it. "If something new occurs or someone frightens you, call me. Also, you'll need to stay away from the crime scene. We've sectioned it off. Do not bypass our tape. I'll be in touch if I have any other questions."

He didn't give her a chance to distract him with more charm and charisma. He simply turned and walked off. "Oh, one more thing, Miss Ladling," he called, glancing at her over his shoulder to steal a final peek. "Don't leave town."

Though she wasn't a suspect at this time, he needed to keep her close and accessible. No one had better knowledge of the property. That he liked the idea, well, he wouldn't examine it too closely.

CHAPTER THREE

A well-tailored suit is perfect for both showing off and hiding your muscles. Which is perfect for distracting anyone in your vicinity.

–A Gravekeeper's Guide to Dating

*C*onrad pulled on a pair of latex gloves as he checked the path outside the old business center for tracks. There. He found a set consistent with the size and tread of the victim's shoes. Which meant Dr. Hotchkins had visited at least once. No evidence of a companion. Yet.

Ancient hinges screamed as the front door swung open. Conrad made his way inside a dim, dusty foyer. Heat swallowed him in an instant, as if he'd entered a human-sized oven. Musty air assaulted his nostrils. Glittering dust motes danced in beams of light that streamed through slats in the boarded windows. Decades of dirt and grime covered everything from rusting metal filing cabinets to scuffed wooden chairs. Cardboard boxes sat piled against one wall. On the other walls hung framed photographs of the cemetery, first in black and white and then full color, depicting the passage of time.

A bookshelf in back contained stacks of loose photos featuring a young Jane Ladling. Some were candid snapshots, while others were more formal school portraits. Picture after picture showcased her sparkling eyes and toothy smile.

He picked up an adorable image of little Jane in front of a doll's casket. She pressed a hand over her heart and pretended to wipe away a tear. *This. Worth the third-degree burns in his lungs.*

Several frames balanced on a spiral album where he discovered even more photos of the fascinating woman as a young girl. The freckles had been more prominent back then, and her hair had often contained flower petals, twigs or leaves. Dirt smudges repeatedly stained her clothes and caked her fingers. She seemed to grow from the land itself.

In most of the photos, she tended a gravesite alongside a younger Fiona or an older couple he'd bet were her grandparents. Why were there no snapshots of her with her mother or father? Had she lost them as a child?

He jolted at the thought. *Focus on the dead body.* Right. Conrad prowled through the rest of the building. By a makeshift coffee station, near the backdoor, he found a clod of fresh dirt, still damp. Fallen from a shoe? Perhaps a shovel? Jane said she rarely ventured here.

Would he find more evidence of fresh dirt on the back porch? He scanned as he moved forward. Hmm. The porch appeared a little too neat and tidy, considering the state of the rest of the center. A clean up? That would indicate, what? The killer had planned ahead and brought supplies? There were usually only two reasons for such pre-planning. Love gone wrong or money.

On the lookout for any signs of foot traffic, he traversed the rear path. The same path the killer might've taken before and/or after doing the dirty deed. There. A partial footprint in a patch between stones. Someone had wiped away most of it but left the faint outline of the toes.

Details hit. A thick tread. Probably from a boot. Smaller than Hotchkins.

He placed an evidence marker to denote the spot, took photos, then hustled to the burial site and sent the forensic photographer to the marker.

Barrow spotted him and ended a call. "Hightower says news of the doctor's death is spreading over a town app known as the Headliner. There's also mention of a rumored affair between Dr. Hotchkins and a patient. Or two."

"Did the sheriff track down the wife?"

"He did. She's at home. He's parked nearby, but he hasn't gone to the door yet. He's waiting for your go ahead."

"Tell him to deliver the news, find out if the doctor's car is parked in the garage, then bring the widow to his office for further questioning." They walked a fine line with spouses, who were both suspects and secondary victims. He'd let Sheriff Moore, a familiar face, handle this one, as long as Conrad could observe.

Barrow made the call while they trekked to the SUV. The closer they came to the cottage, the more Conrad's anticipation mounted. Would he soon enjoy his third encounter with Jane Ladling?

His shoulders rolled in. No sign of her nearby. She must have gone inside.

All right. No big deal. That was that then. So his gaze remained on the front door until the last possible moment, a part of him willing her to exit? So what?

THE SHERIFF'S office surprised Conrad. A junior lieutenant buzzed him past a front counter that looked like it had come from a kitchen in the fifties before escorting him to a room with a cluster of mismatched desks, each acting as a time capsule from its era.

Barrow set up shop at the first empty desk to make more calls. Conrad explored and found a glass-walled conference room around the corner. He draped his jacket over a chair that was tucked into a square table alongside three others and settled in.

He didn't have to wait long. Sheriff Moore arrived with Tiffany Hotchkins. Details about the widow hit Conrad, one after the other. Five nine. Slender and sun kissed. Dark hair in a messy bun. Jane's age. Visibly upset with bloodshot eyes and tear-stained cheeks. Free of makeup. Wearing an orange tank and red shorts with mismatched socks and carrying a fancy designer bag. Had she dressed in a daze? Or on purpose?

Did he detect grief or a fear of getting caught? Both?

As the pair entered the room, Mrs. Hotchkins acknowledged Conrad's presence and sniffled into a tissue. The sheriff made introductions while pulling out a chair on the opposite side of the table. She eased into it, and Moore sat beside her.

"I know this is awful of us to do," the other man began with a pointed look Conrad's way, "but it's gotta be done. We need to know where you were last night."

"I took a pill and passed out, okay?" She pressed her knuckles against her trembling mouth. Tears dripped from her eyes. "I'd just found out my husband cheated on me. That he's been banging a patient for months. A married woman, I might add."

"What's her name?" he asked.

"You tell me. The person who sent me anonymous texts

29

about them said only that she's older than me and super unattractive. Can you believe it? You'd think Marcus could've done me the courtesy of picking someone younger and prettier, so I'd know how I failed to measure up. I hate him so much!" Fresh tears welled, and a whimper escaped. "Or I hated him, past tense. But I didn't want him dead."

As Moore inquired about the witness's identity and obtained the phone number used to send those text, Conrad pondered the new information. The wife had no alibi but plenty of motive. Which, granted, could mean she'd done exactly as she asserted. On the other hand, her blunt honesty could be nothing but a lie. Either way, they needed to speak with the eyewitness who'd contacted her, then the alleged mistress, then the mistress's spouse.

"The doctor's death saves you from a nasty divorce," Conrad stated when the wife failed to offer anything substantial about the informer. He might as well play the role of bad cop.

"You think I don't know that?" Mrs. Hotchkins shouted. "Now I have to live the rest of my life without ever getting revenge. It's not fair!" She crumpled in her seat, silently sobbing in the tissue.

Okay. Conrad had heard a lot of things during interrogations, but that was new.

"He ignored me for so long," she said, sniffling. "Acted as if I meant nothing after I gave up everything for him! He pretended to be obsessed with his stupid treasure hunt. He really sold it, too, pretending to study the clues. Now the truth is so clear. Obviously he used the search for gold as an excuse to see his mistress!"

Hmm. A treasure hunt might explain the unearthing of the coffin. The philandering doctor could've hoped to steal jewelry from the deceased. "Tell us more about the gold."

She swiped at her face, the action jerky. "Why? It's

stupid. I mean, there's always been stories circulating around town about a missing fortune. Every kid in a fifty-mile radius dreams of being the one to find it. Then we grow up. Or some of us do," she added with a bitter tinge. After wiping her nose with the back of her hand, she shook her head, as if attempting to align her thoughts. "Two years ago, the museum decided to celebrate the long-time rumors. Marcus and I donated family journals to the display and attended the opening event. Half the town did. He had no interest until a couple months ago. Something he read in another patron's journals sparked his interest. Or seemed to. Guess that's how he got the idea to cover up his affair."

Was she correct? Had Dr. Hotchkins faked a treasure hunt? Why venture into the cemetery then? "I'd appreciate a look at his notes." A good gold seeker kept good records, right?

"Whatever. You can have them. I don't care anymore. Just find whoever did this and make them forever rot in prison."

"Sheriff Moore will collect everything when he drives you home." Conrad tapped a pen against the table. "Did your husband ever mention a treasure hunting partner?"

"Not by name." With a scowl, Mrs. Hotchkins told him, "He was smart enough to pretend the little hussy was just one of the *bros* so I wouldn't catch on."

Or the partner really was a bro. "Do you know why Marcus visited the Garden of Memories in the middle of the night?" For that matter... "To your knowledge, did he ever visit the Garden before?"

Her nose wrinkled with distaste. "Are you asking if my husband slept with the cemetery girl? Because ew. No. No one is that desperate."

Ew? Desperate? Conrad flicked the tip of his tongue against an incisor. *The widow is a poor judge of character. Noted.*

"Did Marcus have any enemies?" Moore asked, moving on.

"Well, yeah." She slid her red-rimmed glare from one lawman to the other. "The mistress's husband. If you need help figuring out that part, I fear for the rest of this investigation. There's also the person who sent me those anonymous texts, telling me about the affair. In fact, they suggested Marcus had something going with Emma Miller, too. She's a nurse at his clinic."

"I'll need the texter's contact information."

She dug a cell from her purse and rattled off the information. "Oh, and let's not forget Dr. Julian Garcia, co-owner of the clinic, who was impatient to buy Marcus's half. They fought constantly."

Conrad attempted to ask more questions, but she burst into tears. He ended up concluding the interview. Honestly? He wasn't sorry to do it. He doubted he'd get much more from her today.

As soon as he and Moore were alone, Conrad shifted toward the sheriff. "I want a car monitoring the cemetery." If there was indeed a town wide treasure hunt, other citizens might attempt to sneak onto the property, possibly putting Ms. Ladling in danger.

The other man stroked his beard. "With the indomitable Fiona Lawrence on alert, I'm certain the Garden will be just fine."

Did Conrad sense something more than admiration? "Still. I'd like a drive-by every hour."

"I can spare a unit for a few nights, but no longer."

"Do what you can." He hedged for a moment. "Any history between the widow and Jane Ladling?"

"Nothing that I know about. Most townsfolk consider the Ladling girl eccentric. I, myself, would liken her to organized chaos. Lives in a world of her own, that's for sure."

Eccentric? In a world of her own? Perhaps. It made her interesting. But organized chaos? Not even close.

He messaged Hightower, a history buff, to visit the museum, then collected Barrow. As the agent navigated to the Aurelian Hills Medical Clinic, Conrad keyed up the facility's website to read over employee bios and prepare for the interviews to come.

"Not as many cars as I expected," Barrow muttered as he parked.

Only four other vehicles filled the lot. "I'm betting they're closed to the public."

They exited into the heat of the day, then strode inside the one-story building. A spacious lobby sat free of patients. A harried receptionist perched behind a counter, making and fielding calls, canceling all appointments. Conrad made a note to speak with her later.

"We're with Georgia Bureau of Homicide, and we'd like to see Dr. Garcia and Emma Miller," Barrow said, speaking over the ringing and greeting.

Barely glancing up, she pointed to a door. They traversed a wide hallway with multiple closed doors and ended up at the nurse's station, where two women huddled together. He recognized both from their employee photos. Emma Miller, dressed in corgi print scrubs, and a physician's assistant named Caroline Whittington, who wore pale green scrubs.

The redheaded Whittington rubbed Mrs. Miller's back in a gesture of comfort and whispered something Conrad couldn't hear.

Barrow cleared his throat, and both women faced them. Mrs. Miller noticed their badges and paled. She appeared younger in person, displaying a wide-eyed vulnerability that probably demanded a second glance from nearly everyone she encountered. Had the doctor done more than look?

"You're here about Dr. Hotchkins. You heard the rumor,

I'm guessing." Stiffening, Mrs. Miller wiped her tear-stained face. "No, I didn't have an affair with him. No, I didn't kill him."

Ms. Whittington, who bore a tear-stained face as well, patted the woman's shoulder, offering another dose of comfort.

"Before you ask," Mrs. Miller continued, "yes, I fully believe my husband was capable of committing this murder."

He blinked in astonishment. Throwing the spouse under the bus. Another interesting turn. "What makes you think so?"

"Tony gets mean when he drinks, and he's been drinking a ton more than usual since the rumors featuring me and Dr. Hotchkins started up. Last night, we were at home, arguing again." She dabbed at her eyes. "He threatened the doctor's life, then stormed out and never returned. His full name is Anthony Martin Miller, by the way. I can spell it if you'd like."

"That's not necessary." Conrad made a note: *Research the husband. And the wife.*

"You were home alone the rest of the night?" Barrow asked. "Perhaps you spoke with a neighbor?"

"Nope. I stayed home all night and yes, I was alone. I didn't speak with anyone in person. I called Tiffany Hotchkins around ten, though, to tell her Tony might stop by to harass her husband and accuse him of sleeping with me. Which never happened," she reiterated. "Sometime after the call with Tiff, I video chatted with Dr. Garcia concerning a patient who'd been admitted to the hospital earlier in the day. I think the conference lasted two hours."

Two hours discussing the patient and only the patient? Not likely. "Did Mrs. Hotchkins answer your call?" Had the widow not fallen asleep after taking her pill, as stated? Or had she not taken a pill at all?

"She did answer, but she only mumbled incoherently before hanging up."

He'd have a tech at GBH ping the call, see where Mrs. Hotckins's cell signal registered. "Do you and Dr. Garcia often confer about patients in your personal time?"

"No." She shrunk into herself before bowing up, defensive. "But we needed to discuss Dr. Hotchkins as well and figure out how to save the clinic."

Yeah. That tracked.

"There's something you should know," Ms. Whittington piped up. "Dr. Hotchkins *was* sleeping with a few of our patients. Emma caught him with someone last week. She entered the wrong exam room and discovered Dr. Hotchkins in the middle of..." She winced. "You know. Dr. Garcia got involved, and the two men argued. That's when Dr. Hotchkins admitted to, um, servicing other patients."

Mrs. Miller flinched, as if the memory still horrified her.

Conrad sensed another emotion simmering beneath the horror. Anger perhaps? But did it stem from a coworker's ruinous behavior, the accusations launched against her, or something worse?

"Did Dr. Hotchkins ever mention a treasure hunt?" Barrow asked.

"Not this again." The PA released an aggravated groan. "It's amazing how often those silly rumors surface."

"He didn't. Not to me." Going on the defensive, Mrs. Miller grated, "But then, like I've tried to tell you and everyone else, I wasn't involved with him romantically. We spoke on video chats for work when necessary and exchanged nothing but pleasantries before and after office hours."

Protesting a tad too much? He refocused on Whittington. "What do you mean, not this again?"

"Just that every so often locals come in with cuts and

gashes they received while searching for clues about long-lost gold." She pulled a cell from the pocket of her lab coat, checked the screen and frowned. A distressing message? "As for Dr. Hotchkins, I never heard him mention a hunt. Although. Hmm. I did overhear him speaking with someone on the phone the other day. He said something about a nugget. I assumed he was talking about chicken. He also accused the other person of being a lousy partner and demanded the drinking stop." She winced at Mrs. Miller. "Sorry."

Tony Miller, a gold hunter who'd believed the rumors to be real? A killer? "Did you hear the voice on the other line?"

"I didn't, I'm sorry."

No matter.

"Did the call take place on Dr. Hotchkins's cell or the office phone?" Barrow asked.

If the office phone, the receptionist might have recognized the speaker's voice before putting the call through to the doctor.

"Cell," she said, blowing that angle.

Conrad planned to check the records of both phones anyway and do a comparison. If a partner called one line, odds were good he'd called the other line too at some point. "Did the name Jane Ladling come up when Garcia and Hotchkins argued?" A question he asked because he must. Definitely not for any other reason.

The PA's frown returned as she pondered, then she hiked her shoulders in a shrug. "He could have. I'm sorry, but there were just so many names tossed around. I'd have trouble remembering them on an ordinary day, and this is no ordinary day. Everything is currently a blur."

A sensation he knew well.

"Are rumors true for once?" Mrs. Miller croaked. "Was Marcus found at the cemetery?"

Unwilling to respond, Conrad focused on Whittington, saying, "If you recall anyone Dr. Hotchkins mentioned, I'd like to know. Considering the information has nothing to do with their medical history, you should have no problem sharing," he added, hoping to head off a demand for a warrant. Something he *would* obtain, regardless.

"We appreciate it," Barrow told her, handing over his card. He was a bulldog with a bone.

"I can try to put together a list," she hedged, accepting the paper. "Why don't I call you? Or email?"

"Either is fine."

"You'd probably like to speak to Julian about this. Dr. Garcia," she corrected. Dangling bait to get the heat off herself? "He messaged me a moment ago to say he was heading home to grieve his friend. They may have quarreled quite a lot lately, but they liked and admired each other once. I'm sure he'll be eager to help you however he can." She rattled off the man's private cell phone number.

Two things troubled Conrad. Garcia had taken off to grieve after GBH arrived, using a back door. And she defended him almost as much as she detailed reasons for his guilt.

"Thanks for your time," Conrad said with a nod. He and his partner strode off.

As they reached the exit, Whittington caught up with them. "Agents," she whisper-yelled, thrusting a leather-bound book his way. "I didn't want to say anything in front of Emma. Julian and I hope to keep the information to ourselves...we'd hate for more rumors to spread. But Dr. Hotchkins stashed this in his office, using it to keep track of his..." Her lips pursed with distaste. "Conquests. We failed to decipher it. He called it a–" cringed– "buffet. He assigned a food nickname to each woman. A quote unquote dish he kept ready to serve hot. I think the chili pepper grading system is pretty self-explanatory." With that, she dashed off.

Conrad flipped through the offering. A calendar and planner, encased in black leather. Meant to be a type of "little black book"? He skimmed through the entries, spotting a list of the "dishes." *You've got to be kidding me.*

The doctor hadn't even given the women good food names. No, he'd gone with mashed potatoes, corn casserole, fried pickles, and cheeseburger. Oh, look. At least one lucky lady was known as 'carrot cake.'

The doctor had been a tool. Noted.

Conrad and Barrow shared a look before returning to their vehicle. They sat in silence for a bit as the GPS led them out of the town square and toward Dr. Garcia's residence.

Finally Barrow asked, "What do you think?"

"I think our pool of suspects is over-crowded." As for Mrs. Miller and Ms. Whittington, his first impression hadn't yet fully formed. Both showed classic signs of guilt *and* innocence. Which could be explained in a number of ways and teeter in either direction. A thorough search into their private lives should help clear up matters. Though he doubted Whittington was one of the doctor's lovers. Why give them the planner if she were in it?

Conrad typed 'Anthony Martin Miller' into a search engine. The results appeared on his phone's screen, and he groaned. "The nurse's husband is a lawyer." Attorneys made the worst suspects, victims, and witnesses. The worst everything. On the other hand, they excelled at evading interviews and answering questions without giving real information.

"He'll be difficult to pin down," Barrow said with a groan.

"For sure." Conrad dialed the man. No better time to start the game of phone tag. After several rings, voice mail picked up. He left a message, requesting an immediate call back.

They arrived at Dr. Garcia's house. A two-story Victorian

with white shutters. Barrow knocked on the door. Though they waited, no response was forthcoming.

"So much for going home to grieve," Conrad muttered.

"Or he's hiding out inside."

"Either option looks bad."

On the return drive to the office, he phoned the doctor's personal number. Just as he'd done with the attorney, he left a message, requesting a call back–which he received seconds after passing the planner to the right people at GBH headquarters.

"This is Julian Garcia," the doctor began without preamble. "You wished to speak with me."

Grief did lace the man's voice. But so did defensiveness. "Can you tell me what you were doing last night between twelve and four?"

A sharp intake of breath. "You suspect me of killing my associate." A statement, not a question.

"I'm doing my job, ruling out everyone I can." Conrad strove for a reassuring tone.

A huff. Then, "Around seven, I was called to Pinetum Regional Hospital to examine a patient. When I finished there, I grabbed a late dinner with my family at home, then returned to the clinic to write up my notes. I think it was near eleven when I realized I needed information from my nurse to complete my paperwork. I initiated a video call that lasted a couple hours. I left the clinic close to two and engaged the alarm."

The phone must have a timestamp too, and Conrad *would* be verifying everything. "Do you usually phone your employees after hours?"

"No. This was a special circumstance. I originally texted her. She responded. This went on for a while before we agreed to make things easier on ourselves and speak rather than type."

"Where was the nurse located during the call?" And why think she'd know anything about a patient without a file?

"At home. Hers, not mine."

"Did you discuss anything besides the patient?" Would he corroborate Emma's claim?

A pause, then a muffled, "We might have mentioned Marcus. I recently discovered he fathered six children with various women in Atlanta. He's been draining the company account to pay child support. And blackmail, no doubt."

Well, no wonder Hotchkins had (allegedly) taken up treasure hunting. And could this case get any more complicated? How many suspects were they going to unearth in a single day? So far, they had the scorned spouse, multiple angry momma bears, a partner betrayed, and countless lovers and their assortment of vengeful husbands and boyfriends.

After getting the names of the mothers from Garcia, Conrad said, "That's all I need to know for now. Thank you for your time."

They disconnected, and he got busy tracking down the mothers. He also took the necessary steps to obtain a court order for Garcia and Mrs. Miller's phone logs. Conrad read over the field reports as they came in and assigned follow-up tasks to fellow agents. Hours passed. All spent thinking, constantly running scenarios and working theories in the back of his mind.

At some point, a tight-lipped Hightower knocked on his open door. "You got a minute?"

"Do you come bearing news from the museum?"

"I do."

"Then I've got several minutes," he told her, motioning her inside.

She strode over, a notepad in hand, and eased into a chair. "Here's what I learned from the *Gold Fever!* exhibit. Minus information about the spur of economic development caused by the gold rush." Flipping to a specific page, she said, "Most of the documents handed over by the widow seemed to be copies of journal entries on display, written by at least ten different people. Some authors were members of a cult known as the Order of Seven, who'd claimed to find gold. Each hid his stash somewhere in town, using a different code to create a map. What the doctor managed to decipher alluded to nuggets being hidden inside coffins buried at the Garden of Memories. Two museum employees remember seeing Dr. Hotchkins, and confirmed he visited frequently but always alone."

"So it's not likely the treasure hunt was a cover for an affair."

"That's my guess," she said with a nod. "No one recalled spotting Tiffany Hotchkins, Anthony Miller, Emma Miller, Caroline Whittington, Julian Garcia or Jane Ladling at the display."

Adorable freckles, big blue eyes and an outrageous hat popped into his mind, stealing his concentration.

Focus on the dead body, not the brunette.

Easier thought than done. Conrad stood, stretching the kinks from his back. "I'm grabbing a coffee before diving into the backgrounds of our people of interest. You want one?"

Hightower glanced at the clock showing 11:11 p.m. "Go home, Ryan. Get some rest. That's what I'm doing." She closed the notepad and also stood. "You'll be no good to anyone if you fall asleep on your feet tomorrow. Trust me, it's the best way to tick off Randall and earn grunt duty."

So late already? He'd lost track of time. Though the thought of going home and pretending to rest held no appeal. No matter how hard Conrad tried, he couldn't sleep. And it wasn't like he had any family, pets, or plants in need of tending. He had no real friendships outside of Wyatt Murray, his foster brother. But Conrad did have a recording of the Hawks game. That should help pass the time at least. And keep his mind off a charming vision in purple and her menacing cat.

"You're right. I'll walk you out." He escorted Hightower to the parking garage, drove home...and gathered intel all night, the game forgotten. The quicker he solved this case, the sooner he could take a certain groundskeeper to dinner. And serve justice to a cold-blooded killer, of course.

The next morning, Conrad beat everyone to the office. He put investigators to work as soon as they arrived, pushing them to the limit with his demands for information. Where was the autopsy report? Why hadn't the court orders come in yet?

"You're grouchier than normal," his boss remarked after a quick briefing.

"My apologies." He *was* gruffer than usual and wouldn't waste time denying it. He rubbed a hand along the back of his neck. "I'm eager to close this one."

"You always are. What's different now?"

Miss Ladling's visage popped into his head once again. "Everything? Nothing?" Only time would tell.

CHAPTER FOUR

Try not to hide your gooey center beneath a hard candy shell. A girl can keep herself from taking a bite for only so long.

–A Gravekeeper's Guide to Dating

*C*onrad planned to drive to Aurelian Hills after completing a series of interviews with the doctor's baby mommas. If he happened to stop by the cemetery, well, that was simply part of his due diligence, right? But only fifteen minutes into the first conference, Barrow knocked over a mug of lukewarm coffee, soaking Conrad's pants, making him look as if he'd peed himself.

Left with no other choice, he returned home to shower and change. What were the chances the autopsy report came in while he was out of the office?

As he wiped steam off his bathroom mirror, he noticed a missed call on his cell, from a number he didn't recognize. Mr. Miller finally ready to talk?

Conrad pressed play, only to jolt when a familiar feminine voice emanated from the speaker.

"Hi Conrad. It's Jane. Jane Ladling. From Garden of Memories." Pause. "The cemetery." Pause. "In Aurelian Hills." Pause. "Where the murder occurred. Ringing any bells? Hello. Um, I'm calling to ask if you've made any progress with the case. I haven't heard from you, but seeing how the crime occurred on my property, I should probably be kept in the loop. Maybe? The crime scene tape is still intact, by the way. Not that I'm double checking every couple of minutes. Okay bye!"

He added her name to his contact list and decided to call her back as soon as he had information he could share. Or his will power failed, whichever came first. But honestly, he couldn't stop smiling on the inside.

Conrad returned to GBH headquarters to learn the coroner's report hadn't come in but Barrow and Hightower had completed the rest of the interviews. Forget the trip to Aurelian Hills. He needed to watch over the recorded feed. Which meant he might be looking at an all-nighter.

Hightower knocked on his door soon after he settled into his chair, her lips pressed into a thin line. "Someone spray painted a fleur-de-lys sign on multiple cars in Aurelian Hills. Many of the owners are associates of our victim."

"Do you have pictures?"

"I do." She stepped inside, placing a sheaf of paper on his desk, each depicting an expensive vehicle desecrated with three distinctive neon-blue petals joined at their base. "The quality is grainy because I downloaded the images from the message board the locals use. Good news is, the sheriff's office is investigating, and we can piggyback off their findings."

"Any idea why the artist chose a fleur-de-lys?"

She nodded. "The same symbol was used by the Order of Seven. It's found in several of the journal entries at the museum."

The fine hairs along the back of his neck stood at attention. Why do this? Why point to the treasure hunt at all—unless this was an attempt at misdirection? What if the murder had nothing to do with the treasure and everything to do with the affairs?

"Call the sheriff and offer your assistance. Insist on it," he commanded. "I want to know what's found, when it's found."

Hightower nodded, turned on her heel and left.

Conrad watched one interview after another, then made calls and verified alibis. Lots and lots of alibis. An arduous but necessary progress. Most checked out. Some didn't.

His team hadn't yet deciphered the full list of women in Hotchkins's planner. The "buffet." Thankfully the PA had emailed the names the doctor mentioned to Dr. Garcia. Those he'd verbally admitted to sleeping with. Whittington had added 'Jane Ladling' at the bottom, next to the only notation. *Dr. Garcia doesn't remember her specifically, but he says he can't rule her out, either, because Dr. Hotchkins did mention visiting the cemetery recently.*

Jane had not cited any such visit. Which meant Hotchkins had made the visit in secret. Conrad hadn't changed his mind about the gravekeeper. She was a hundred percent on the up and up. No way the cupcake had lied or committed such a violent act. The cat, on the other hand... now there was a possible killer.

Snickering, he reclined in his chair. Tucked away in his private office, he allowed his thoughts to veer deeper in Jane's direction. What was she doing right this second? Should he return her call? Or ask her to come in for an official interview?

The tension in his shoulders eased as he warmed up to the idea. What would she think of his workspace? He imagined her cottage stuffed with hats and cat toys. Based on his observations of the old business center, Ladlings loved family photos. Did images consume her private walls?

Hmm. He'd never bothered to hang any pictures here. Just certificates. Not a single frill anywhere, in fact, which was precisely the way he liked it. Or thought he'd like it. Guess it depended on the decorator.

A new knock sounded at the door. Conrad sat up a little too quickly, as if he'd gotten caught doing something he shouldn't. He pursed his lips before calling, "Come in."

Barrow entered, saying, "Got the coroner's report." The agent strode over to drop the file on the desk. "Narrowed the time of death to somewhere between one fifteen and one forty-five."

"Excellent. Thank you. Hopefully we can use the information to expedite a meeting with Mr. Miller." Who still hadn't returned his call. With that thought, he forgot about Barrow and dove into the file.

Cause of death: severed aorta via broken rib. So. Not the blunt force trauma to the head Conrad had expected. Though the doctor *had* suffered a severe skull fracture. Possible weapon: something small, metal and heavy, with a sharp edge. Most likely scenario: blow to the temple, six feet fall and crash into the coffin. The broken ribs occurred on impact. He'd died seconds later.

No foreign fibers were found on the body. Nothing but dirt under his fingernails. Because why make things easy?

He picked up a pen and crafted a possible timeline of events.

Roughly 6:30 p.m., Dr. Hotchkins arrives home. Fights with his wife about his affairs.

Close to 8:00, he shuts himself in his office to study treasure hunt notes.

9:45, wife believes he's still inside the office. She turns on the security system and takes a sleeping pill.

At exactly 10:33, the security system is disabled.

There were no incoming or outgoing calls or texts on Dr. Hotchkins's phone at the time—which indicated he'd planned his excursion. Further proof: he'd left his phone at home. He must have had a second device no one had found... because the killer had taken it.

Those footprints circling the old business center and the cleanliness of the porch continued to intrigue Conrad. Clearly something had gone down there. But had that something occurred at the hands of a jealous husband, a fed-up colleague, or a scorned lover?

1:15- 1:45. The killer strikes Dr. Hotchkins.

6:30. Jane finds the body.

Killer had plenty of time to clean the entire Garden.

Conrad rubbed tired, burning eyes, then reached for his mug of coffee. Empty again.

Knock, knock. "Did you ever go home?" Barrow asked.

Chin jerking up, Conrad spotted his fresh-faced partner in the doorway. The agent must have gone home—and brought a new morning with him upon his return.

Conrad had been at his desk all night, going over files?

"You look like crap," the other man announced.

"Wrong. I look like determination." He scrubbed a hand over his stubbly jaw before returning his focus to the paperwork. "I will finish organizing my thoughts or die trying."

A sigh. Footsteps. A soft snick. Alone again. Conrad's mind whirled. Tiffany Hotchkins, Emma Miller, and Anthony Miller remained strong people of interest. But so did many—many—others. The doctor had helped destroy a myriad of families, yet he'd also seemed genuinely obsessed with his treasure hunt. But who had aided his search?

Did Jane know about the Order of Seven stuff? Had she beefed up security as promised? Conrad really should check in on her. What wild things would the gravekeeper's say today? And she was right. He did regret not eating those blueberry pancakes when he'd had the chance.

His stomach twisted with sudden hunger. He was in the process of standing, intending to grab a blueberry muffin from the breakroom, when his cell rang. The screen flashed the name Jane Ladling, and he flopped back down, already grinning.

His voice dipped as he answered, "Special Agent Ryan."

"Hi. Hello. I was calling to see if you've interviewed Tiffany Hotchkins. The wife." The words burst from her in a continuous stream, never giving him a chance to respond. "Tiffany is certain her husband had an affair with tons of locals. Abigail Waynes-Kirkland might or might not have been one of those women. Apparently, Dr. Hotchkins gave, um, vitamin D injections in exam rooms. Um...you know what that means right? Anyway, most of the women are single, but some are married. You'll want to investigate their spouses too probably. I have a list of names and descriptions." Something crackled over the line. A piece of paper she held?

Laughter brewed on his tongue. Vitamin D injections, spoken with her sweet, southern drawl. She could not be more adorable. He couldn't help but tease her, "Jane Ladling?"

"Right. Sorry." She audibly winced. "Yes, this is Jane Ladling. Why don't I start over?" Deep breath in. Out. "Have you interviewed Dr. Hotchkins's wife? Or her friend, Abigail Waynes-Kirkland?"

Well, well, well. Talk about instant clarity for Conrad. Jane was a hardcore Hallmark fanatic, wasn't she? Ready to live her own small-town adventure or something similar. The quirky gravekeeper turned amateur sleuth. A story he now kind of really wanted to watch. He was only ashamed to admit he hadn't figured out the truth sooner. All the clues had been there. The unconventional setting. Her fellow offbeat cast of characters, including an older grandmother type and a beloved pet with quirks of his own.

For her safety, Conrad had better nip this plotline in the bud and share as little as possible. "I'm currently pursuing several people of interest. That's all I can tell you."

"Am I still one of those people?"

Ding, ding, ding. Amateur sleuth out to clear her good name. And why—how!—did this rouse even more delight in him?

Words rolled from his tongue, low and throaty. "There's definite interest in you here at the bureau, Jane."

A strangled sound left her, as if she didn't quite understand his meaning. Then a new burst of information spewed from her. "There's something else you should know. Dr. Hotchkins's nurse may or may not be one of the women who may or may not have had an affair with him. I'm not sure yet."

"Yet?" He'd nipped nothing, apparently. The idea of Jane deliberately putting herself in the path of a killer prodded his deepest protective instincts. Time to get stern. "Do not question anyone or dig into the case, Jane. That's my job. Do you understand?"

She sputtered for a moment. "Look, you missed a wild scene at the Hotchkins's house this morning. Tiffany accused everyone of sleeping with her husband. Emma Miller, his nurse, rushed out crying and sped away. I even heard that Dr. Hotchkins argued with his staff the day before his murder. Don't you find that the tiniest bit suspicious?"

The sleuth is strong in this one.

Had Mrs. Miller lied about sleeping with Dr. Hotchkins or not? A question for later. Right now, Conrad needed to deal with Jane. Maybe he should shine the light of guilt on *her*, forcing her to back down? "What I find suspicious is your visit to the widow of a victim found on your property. A man you claim you've never spoken with. Why would you do that?"

"Because it's polite." Her scolding tone should not delight him. No, it definitely should not. "I didn't know the doctor, but I went to high school with Tiffany." A cat screamed bloody murder in the background. "Someone has to solve the crime, put a murderer away, and clear the good names of the innocent."

Nope, shining the light of guilt on her had been the worst route imaginable. "That's right. Someone has to, and it's me. Trust me on this. I'm working as fast as humanly possible."

"Everyone needs help now and then," she told him with the firm but merciful tone of a patient teacher with an unruly grade school student, "and you could certainly use mine. You wouldn't have this lead about Dr. Hot's nurse without me. You're welcome, by the way."

He would never be able to coral her, would he? "I'm going to pretend I didn't hear you call him by that ridiculous nickname. And I've been looking into the clinic employees since day one."

"Well?" she demanded, all but daring him to prove his smarts. "Have you found anything?"

He heaved a sigh. Soooo badly he wanted to spill what he knew. Only thing he could do? Repeat, "I'm pursuing several people of interest." For his own peace of mind, he changed the subject. "Did you get someone out there to beef up security?"

"I called a local business from...mmm...Peach State Security. Yes, that's it. We haven't managed to connect, though. Apparently he just opened up shop. I'm going to give him a couple more days."

A few days? Not good enough. "I instructed Sheriff Moore to have a deputy patrol the cemetery each night, but he doesn't have the resources to spare the man much longer. Nor do I." If Conrad had to spend the next few nights parked in front of her cottage, he would. "If you don't hear back from Peach State Security by the end of business today, let me know. I'm acquainted with several firefighters here in Atlanta who install security equipment on their off days."

"Okay, will do," she said as a muffled knock drifted to his ears. "Gotta go. I've got a visitor. No doubt it's someone else wanting a peek at the crime scene. Don't worry, though. Rolex and I are taking care of it." *Click.*

Conrad pursed his lips and stared down at his phone. Organized chaos. He saw it now. She was Hurricane Jane, both the wind and eye of the storm.

Throughout the day, as sense of bemusement blazed brighter and brighter. He decided to shelve his work for the evening, take a break, and start fresh in the morning. Maybe he'd have better results then.

At home, Conrad changed into shorts and tennis shoes, and strapped his phone to his bicep. He headed to Piedmont Park to jog. The hilly paved trail offered the perfect challenge; he lost himself along the Active Oval while listening to a little league ballgame in the distance, then spiked his heart rate by sprinting up and down the stairs. Sweat covered him.

Again and again, his thoughts returned to Jane. Awareness and uneasiness grew, sensitizing his nerve endings. Besides her bootleg investigating, how else did the gravekeeper spend her time? Was it the single purple hat or did she have more? How good were those blueberry pancakes? And why did any of this matter?

He'd only met the woman once and spoken with her twice. He shouldn't be this obsessed. But he was, and he didn't like it. On the other hand, he liked it. A lot.

What was he going to do about this? About *her*? What *should* he do?

By the time he strode into his condo an hour and a half later, he'd burned off some excess energy and none of his inner agitation. He craved a hit of Jane's peace and—noises spilled from his kitchen.

He sighed. No need to grab the gun he'd locked in his safe. He knew the identity of his visitor. Only two people had a key and a free pass from the doorman. But only one of those people ever stopped by unannounced.

Yep. Sure enough. Wyatt puttered about the kitchen, opening cabinets and grunting with disgust. He was younger than Conrad and roughly the same height. A hazel eyed, sandy-haired playboy who was still a kid at heart, with no real emotional armor. He always looked for the best in every person. Something Corbin had done too. Perhaps the reason Conrad had been drawn to him as kids.

With Wyatt, Conrad got to be a big brother again. The pain of losing his family in a car accident didn't hurt as much. Even if it was an all too brief reprieve.

He leaned against the doorframe and waited. At last, Wyatt noticed him and straightened.

The other man spread his arms, unabashed. "You need to go grocery shopping, bro. I'm here to celebrate getting back together with my girl by pillaging from your coffers, but all you've got is a bottle of ketchup and protein shakes."

"I've been busy," he said with a shrug. "Why are you celebrating with me and not her, anyway?"

"Because I already celebrated with her, and I missed you. By the way, I'm ordering us a couple pizzas and you're paying. It's the least you can do since I'm here honoring you with my presence."

Conrad snorted. Thing was, the guy wasn't wrong. "Deal." He grabbed a glass and filled it with water at the sink. "In return, you can give me some romantic advice." No one had dated around more than Wyatt. Although, granted, none of his relationships had ever stuck.

"Whoa, whoa, whoa." Grinning, Wyatt snatched the glass from his hand, water sloshing over the rim. "Romantic advice? Who are you and what have you done with my big bro?"

I don't know! That was kind of what Conrad needed help figuring out. "There's this woman. Jane..."

CHAPTER FIVE

Treat your mysterious past like bait. Dangle tidbits here and there to keep the fish of the sea biting.
–A Gravekeeper's Guide to Dating

The next day, Conrad threw himself into his work. He chased leads, checked more alibis, and drove to and from Aurelian Hills for in-person interviews. He never connected with Anthony Miller–they merely played phone tag–but the team pieced together enough clues to identify a handful of nicknames found in Hotchkins's planner.

Emma Miller wasn't among them–yet. But they *had* learned the doctor had followed the same script with all his women. Same time, same motel, same room. He'd worked out a long-standing deal with a clerk there. That clerk had identified Mrs. Miller as a semi-frequent guest. And a liar.

But, though she'd outright denied the affair, she *had* told the truth about calling Tiffany and speaking with Garcia on her personal computer the night of the murder. The discussion between boss and nurse had lasted two hours and eighteen minutes, to be exact, putting the nurse at home and Garcia at the office at the time of Hotchkins's death.

But. Though Emma and Garcia were each other's alibis, they couldn't prove they'd remained in front of their computers the entire length of the video. They could have banded together to rid themselves of a common enemy: Leave the chat room open to create a digital record, sneak into the cemetery, and boom, murder Hotchkins.

A wild theory, yes, but something Conrad planned to keep on a shelf in his mind for further study.

So far Jane's name had *not* graced the pages of the planner.

Instead of working all night, he went home and watched his cell, hoping for another call from her. To his surprise, the gravekeeper phoned Sheriff Moore bright and early the next morning, Conrad's day off. The sheriff then called him. She thought she'd found the murder weapon. Of course, she didn't know Dr. Hotchkins died due to his fall. Conrad suspected she'd discovered the object used to crack open the victim's skull. In only a matter of minutes, he would question her about it face to face.

A now recognizable anticipation prickled the back of his neck as he parked the sedan in front of her cottage. He emerged into the afternoon light, anchored an arm of his sunglasses inside the neckline of his T-shirt, and walked toward the porch. As he scaled the steps, the door opened, gifting him with a new glimpse of Jane Ladling.

Punch. She stood in the gaping doorframe, wearing a yellow dress, reminding him of a ray of sunshine. Any lingering agitation got knocked smooth out of him. That sweet peace returned, and he breathed deep for the first time in days.

"Welcome back," she burst out, as if she could suppress the words no longer. She might have just curtseyed.

Fighting a grin, he nodded and strode past her, entering the cottage. Conrad looked around. Well-worn and well-loved described her home perfectly. His dress shoes should have clacked against the hardwood floors, but the living area was packed with too much sound deadening stuff. Framed photos, amateur paintings and art from at least four different decades graced the wall.

She moved around him and eased upon the floral print couch with the grace of a debutante. Fiona Lawrence occupied a rocker near the hearth, with a lap full of yarn and two knitting needles in hand. Such a homey picture they presented.

Needing a moment to recover, he focused on the older woman.

"Good afternoon, Fiona. Good to see you again." The woman had tried to insert herself into his personal life and set him up on a date. Forget formalities.

Rolex jumped from the couch and sashayed over, perching at his feet and staring up at him with big yellow beseeching eyes. Their one-sided war had ended? So soon?

Conrad bent down to scratch the little warrior behind the —with a hiss, Rolex clawed his hand hard and fast, leaving two round punctures with jagged tails. Blood welled, and Conrad swallowed a snort. "Good to see you, too, Rolex," he called as the feline bounded off.

Fiona waved the needles in his direction. "Are you trying to charm me into whipping up my blueberry pancakes, young man?" Humphing, the older woman returned her attention to her knitting. "Aw. You poor thing. Your request is denied for reasons." She paused before oh, so sweetly adding, "Unless you ask real polite."

"Ask real polite," Jane beseeched him. "Please, Conrad." She pressed her hands together, assuming a classic begging stance. "There's always time for pancakes."

Regret swamped him. "I'm sorry, but I'm on the clock." The moment his boss approved his request to pick up the weapon, his day off had become a day on. He simply hadn't changed out of his T-shirt and jeans.

Jane's features crumbled, misery radiating from her, and oh, he wanted to kick himself. A disappointed Fiona shook her head at him, as if he'd failed a grade-altering test. Well, then. He'd just have to earn extra credit.

Conrad winked at the matchmaker and motioned to the yarn. "What are you making?"

"They're called funny bunnies." Another humph. This one seemed to be directed at herself. She lifted a perfect wool white rabbit, missing only the tip of an ear. "We donate them to different charities for children. Places that help kids who've lost everything. This might be the only toy the little darlings have for a while."

A barbed lump congealed in his throat. Once upon a time, he'd been that traumatized kid who'd lost everything, surrounded by others who'd lost even more. Acts of kindness, rare as they'd been, had always turned his despair into hope, if only for a little while.

"You're making a difference in a kid's life," he said, his fingers migrating to the tattoos on his forearm. "That's...nice."

Jane blinked at him as if she wasn't sure how to respond.

Not face her fully? Impossible. He turned into her, breathing in a bouquet of honeysuckle and roses, magnolia, and gardenia he might have missed with every fiber of his being. Their gazes met. Locked. Different emotions glinted in her eyes. A whirlwind of confusion, excitement, worry and resolve. And yet, her air of tranquility never lessened. He remained rooted in calm.

"Would you like some sweet tea, Conrad?" she asked

primly, only to slide into a short, harried ramble. "Agent? Special Agent? Special Agent Ryan."

He'd made her nervous again. But it had nothing to do with fear, he realized. *She is aware of me, too.*

"No, thank you, Jane." A ribbon of satisfaction unfurled deep inside him. His eyelids grew heavy. "And it's Conrad, remember?"

Her lips parted, and she shivered. Between one breath and the next, she jolted, as if in the grips of a terrible panic. In a frenzy of motion, she hurried to the empty rocker near the hearth.

So. He intrigued her, but she didn't *want* him to intrigue her. Why?

Taking pity on them both, he asked, "And what are *you* making?"

"Mine is also a bunny." Nose wrinkled, she tapped her toy with the tip of a needle. "Obviously."

"Ah, yes. *Obviously.*" He envied the kid who won her amalgamation of mythological beasts; he really did. It was a true one of a kind collector's item. "The ears are quite... noticeable. And the colors..."

She brightened. "I know! I wasn't sure pink, orange, and red would go together, but the end result is utterly stunning." Chewing on her bottom lip, she gripped the "bunny" by its hunched shoulders and made it dance in the air. "I'll make one for you to remember me by. Or because it's the polite thing to do. Yes, that one. Because I'm polite."

Oh, he intended to own one of her creatures all right, but not because of a gesture of good will. She would give it to him because she'd crafted it specifically for him. An event he anticipated more than he should. And why did he want to pound his fists against his chest gorilla-style?

Fighting a wry grin at his uncharacteristic urges, he said, "I wouldn't want to deprive a kid of their only toy. Maybe you can teach me to knit so I can contribute to the haul." Wait. He was making plans for the future? Before the case was solved?

Right. He was here for a reason. *Focus on the dead body, not the brunette.* He crossed his arms. "So, you think you've found the murder weapon?"

Jane veered from panic to serenity in a split second. "Yes. Beau and I discovered a crowbar as we walked the grounds."

A crowbar fit the size and shape of Dr. Hotchkins's head wound. "Is Beau another pet?"

"Beau is not." Affection softened her expression. "He's the owner of Peach State Security. A long-lost and recently found friend. We went to school together."

As she spoke, a muscular man in his late twenties strode from the hallway. Out of habit, and yes, curiosity, Conrad catalogued his appearance. Green eyes. Blond hair, wet around the edges, and damp skin, as if he'd splashed his face. Or taken a shower. Though he said nothing, aggression emanated from him.

Their gazes clashed, and Conrad stiffened. In that moment, he recognized a rival for the gravekeeper's affections. A development he did not like.

One background check, coming up.

"That's me." Muscles wiped his hands together as he stopped at Jane's side. "I'm Beau Harden."

Conrad looked between the two, his eyelids narrowing. Did Jane return her friend's romantic interest? Impossible to tell. Beaming, she batted her lashes at one man, then the other, those baby blues flashing.

"You're staying with Jane?" he asked the other guy. He ground his molars. All night?

"When requested." Determination roughened Harden's tone. He wiped the moisture from his brow. "And when needed."

Warning received. The rival was here to stay, in one capacity or another, and he expected Conrad to tuck tail and run. Too bad. He was already hooked. He'd tasted of peace, and he was determined to experience more.

"That is magnanimous of you." A truthful statement no lawyer could use against him.

"Isn't it?" Beau asked.

A hiss sounded between them. Jane jumped up and rushed over, shouldering her way between them and the cat.

"Like I was saying," she kind of shouted, "Beau was with me when I spotted the crowbar. I asked him to stick around in case you needed a statement."

He knew Jane had given a statement to Sheriff Moore over the phone. The sheriff had told him all about it. Well, not all. The man had failed to mention a companion. "Just need your current address for now." He withdrew a notebook while Beau rattled off the details. "A statement won't be necessary at this time, Mr. Harden. You are free to leave."

Shoulders rolling in, Jane cried, "I'm sorry I wasted your time, Beau. Please add every second to my bill."

He glanced at Conrad, sending a very clear message. He'd be back. "No problem." The guy approached the couch and hefted a tool bag over his shoulder, then strode to the door, exiting without another word.

Conrad watched Jane as she smiled and waved at her friend. No expanding pupils. No blushes. No romantic interest in the other man? One could hope. "Why don't you take me to the weapon?"

She brightened further, as if thrilled to contribute to the case. "Yes, of course. I'll just be a moment."

"A hat?" *Please be a hat.*

Sassy sweet, she hiked a shoulder, saying, "What can I say? I protect my skin in style." Then she dashed off, and he chuckled.

"Not the purple one. Or the black," Fiona called. "To be safe, pick none of them."

Ahhh, so there were *many* other hats. "What do you not like about the headgear?"

"Everything." Demeanor growing serious, the older woman rolled to her feet and hastened him to the porch. As soon as the door closed, she whispered fiercely, "Let me give you a piece of advice, young man. Figure out what you want before you approach the dessert table. That little cinnamon roll you're devouring with your gaze has raisins. If you aren't willing to put in the work and dig them out, you're unworthy of enjoying such a fine dining experience."

He...had no idea how to respond to that. "Raisins are bad in this analogy?

She snorted. "Raisins are bad in any analogy, sugar. Keep up."

Okay, so raisins were...what? Hidden hurts? "Why can't I stare through the window of the shop until I'm ready to make a purchase?"

"I think we both know the answer to that. Another customer will swoop in and grab your dessert."

He pressed his tongue to the roof of his mouth. Yeah, he could guess the identity of this other customer. "If I lick the cinnamon roll, is it mine?"

She wagged her finger toward his face, her dark eyes fierce. "Now you listen up. If you make her cry, I will use my knitting needles to unman you, understand?"

"If I make her cry," he told her with a flat tone, "I'll deserve it."

"Well then." A new smile bloomed, the animosity seeping from the older woman. "That's comforting to hear. Comforting indeed. You might be the right patron for the job, after all."

Footsteps reached his ears. Must have reached Fiona's too. They both went silent. Seconds later, hinges squeaked.

"I'm ready." Jane stepped outside, drawing his gaze.

The hat. Wow. Bigger than the last one, and the same yellow as her dress, with strings hanging from ragged edges. How absolutely perfect.

"Please." He motioned toward the cemetery, eager to get her alone. "Lead the way."

As they headed off, Fiona called, "Don't forget what I told you, agent."

As if he would ever look at cinnamon rolls or raisins the same way again.

"What did she tell you?" Jane squeaked with wide eyes.

Worried he'd learned something she didn't want him to know? He tried to put her at ease without giving away anything vital. "Several things. The most memorable is the threat to castrate me if ever I'm mean to you."

"Awww." She pressed her hand over her heart. "How sweet is she?"

"The sweetest," he told her, his tone dry, and Jane laughed. Amusement lit her entire face, stealing his breath. Before the day ended, he must hear that tinkling sound again. "She also offered me a bit of advice."

"And?" she prompted.

He boiled the conversation down in a nutshell. "Vague idea, vague results." Know what you want and fight for it or lose by default.

Confusion contorted Jane's delicate features. "What does that mean? Vague idea regarding what?"

"What I want." Or rather, *who* he wanted.

Delight and nervousness battled for domination of her features. Guessed a bit of his meaning? The nervousness won, and she changed the subject. "Will any of the other investigators be joining us?"

"Wanted to check things out myself before bringing a unit here." Plus, he'd been halfway to Aurelian Hills when the call came in. He'd decided to have a meal in town and eavesdrop on the locals. For the good of the case.

"Do you know why fleur-de-lys signs are being spray painted on vehicles?" Jane asked.

Anything he knew, he wasn't allowed to share. "Tell me more about the tours you conduct."

She smiled again. "Do you want to know the different kinds I give? What areas of the cemetery I highlight? A list of those who have recently attended?"

"Everything." Maybe not only for the case.

She launched into a story that centered around the gold rush. Unfortunately, she never mentioned the Order of Seven. Because he was unable to site the cult outright–a detail they were holding close to the vest–he tried to steer her in that direction without being obvious. But all too soon an easy back and forth developed, and he forgot the case entirely. When a light wind blew past, she clasped the edges of her hat, and he lost track of everything else—only his companion registered.

Did she have any idea how beautiful she was? A well of water to a man suddenly aware he was dying of thirst.

"What do you do out here? Exactly," he clarified. He thought he saw her calming effect in every tree and stone.

"For starters, I inherited caretaking duties from my Grandma Lily."

Finally he asked the question he wished to know most. "What happened to your parents?"

"Both are gone."

Sympathy flooded him. Was the loss part of the hurt Fiona hinted at? "I'm sorry. I know the pain of losing your family. I was ten when I lost mine." The words left him of their own accord, shocking him. He never spoke of his family with anyone, yet he'd just casually tossed out the truth with Jane.

She pressed a hand over her heart. "Oh, Conrad. That must have been horrible for you. But, um, I meant neither of them live in Aurelian Hills. Or even Georgia, for that matter. They had me while in high school. My father moved to New Mexico instead of marrying my mom. He's never really been part of my life. My mother wasn't ready for me either, I guess, so Grandma Lily raised me."

Ouch. Her parents might not have died in a tragic accident, but she'd lost them nonetheless. "Pain is pain."

She chewed on her bottom lip before asking, "Who ended up raising you?"

"The system." He left it at that but honestly? Even offering that much information was an oddity for him. But even more surprising was his longing to divulge more. Would she understand? "Your mom isn't part of your life anymore?"

"She is, and she isn't. When I was three, she relocated to Alabama. She took me with her and tried to be a mother, but she struggled. In the end, she shipped me back to Grandma Lily for the summer, and I never left. Now Mom is married and living in Texas with my two half-sisters. She calls me sometimes."

The barest hint of anguish simmered in her undertone. Deep inside him, anger sparked. At least Conrad had known abundant, unwavering love before the death of his mother. Jane had experienced only rejection from hers.

He shoved his hand in his pocket to stop himself from hugging her.

Hug someone? Conrad? What was this woman doing to him? "And your dad?" he asked as gently as possible.

"He's not a dad to me but a father," she said, the anguish more pronounced. "He has another family, an ex-wife and three grown sons." She waved a hand through the air. "And that's a wrap on the story of Jane Ladling. We should probably concentrate on the case. That is why you're here, and the weapon is around the next corner."

The sympathy welled anew.

They passed a wrought iron arch, entering an area teeming with flowers. Sheriff Moore stood near a headstone shaped like a dog. For the second time in their acquaintance, their journey had ended far too soon.

Conrad stopped and met Jane's gaze. "Thank you for the escort." Though he wished to linger, it was time to become a special agent.

She smiled at him, understanding, then turned and promptly sneezed. He almost grinned, charmed all over again as she walked away muttering about not being sick.

Solve the case, focus on the girl.

CHAPTER SIX

Learn to flash a lopsided smile on command. It disarms
anyone with a pulse
–A Gravekeeper's Guide to Dating

*C*onrad read over details he'd gleaned about Beauregard Harden. Decorated war vet, special forces, and an expert at digital security. No traffic tickets. Once pulled an elderly widow from a burning car. All together a pretty decent guy, if you liked heroes.

Right now, Conrad wasn't sure he did.

When his phone dinged, he glanced at the clock. Wow. After midnight already?

Frowning, he reached for the cell and discovered a report on the crowbar he'd retrieved from the cemetery had come in. The weapon was definitely used on Dr. Hotchkins. Trace amounts of his blood dotted one end, but there were no fingerprints. Even still, this provided sufficient reason for Ms. Randall to approve the extra funds needed for surveillance of the graveyard's resident guard dog, Muffin. Or rather, his headstone.

The cell rang, flashing Jane's name over the screen. Worry flared. To call him so late, something must have happened. A little too quickly, Conrad pressed the right button and jammed the phone against his ear. "Jane? Is something wrong?"

"You're a tasty little snack cake. Did you know that?" She both slurred and purred the words before unleashing a hacking cough.

He cringed at the atrocious sound. Then his brow furrowed. Had she actually called him a snack cake? Uh, was she drunk? "Where are you? What's going on?"

"I'm at home in bed. I took some cold medicine, even though I didn't need it," she grumbled. A sneezing fit followed her claim, then another coughing fit, and his trepidation morphed into amusement. "Fiona says I'm a diaper baby and rage monster when I'm sick, so it's a good thing I'm not sick. By the way, colds are dumb, and I'll feed you your own organs if you ever disagree. Oh! You should bring me Daisy's. Okay, bye!"

He stared at his wall for a solid minute, baffled and bemused. In the end, he chuckled with a delightful realization. Jane Ladling couldn't handle her meds. He only hoped he received another call. Soon. There was nothing inappropriate about it, either. He couldn't help when people reached out.

Less than an hour later, his wish came true. His phone rang, and he shoved his laptop aside in favor of snatching up the device. "Hello, Jane." He settled in for the long haul, getting comfortable against the mound of pillows behind him. A smile spread wide.

"I just remembered you never told me the answer," she began, more slurred and nasally than before.

"What was the question?"

"How come you're such a smoke show?"

He barked out a laugh, and there was no stopping it. First a snack cake, now a smoke show. "You like the look of me, do you?" And okay, yes, it was an inappropriate query, but he'd stopped caring.

"Almost as much as Daisy's."

Okay. Hint taken. "Who or what is Daisy?"

"Only the best diner in this world and possibly the galaxy. Did you know the chicken noodle soup cures incurable diseases? Not that I'm sick."

He stored the diner information in a mental folder titled *Jane Ladling: A Survival Guide.* "Tell me about your last boyfriend."

"He's a fireman." She yawned. "His name starts with a C like yours. Guess that's my kryptonite."

"C names do it for you, hmmm?" he teased. "Why'd you two break up?"

"Because he's a liar and liars should only ever be with other liars. I, sir, am not a liar." Her fatigue seemed to evaporate in a flood of vim and vigor. "Am I saying *liar* too much? Anyway. Honesty is a treasure more valuable than gold. Christopher told me he'd stick like glue, but he didn't. At the tenth or eleventh sign of trouble, he bailed. So good riddance, if you ask me. Loyalty is a treasure more valuable than, well, more gold."

A puzzle piece clicked into place. Abandonment issues— raisins. No wonder Fiona had warned him away. The wise older woman must have sensed Conrad's own vast array of problems. "Is that Beau guy a sticker?"

"I hope so, 'cause I've always wanted a brother. Oh! Conrad! Guess what? I'm setting Beau up with a great girl. Well, as soon as I find the right one I am. Oh! Guess what else? I know the answer to everything and it's something."

Brother, she'd said. Relief poured through Conrad. "Congratulations. What are your top three dating deal breakers?"

Another yawn crackled over the line, her burst of energy fading. "Don't hang up," she commanded, the words slurred again. She must have forgotten his question. "I don't want to be alone for once."

He knew the feeling well. "I won't hang up. You have my word."

Rustling. Smacking lips. "You should call me sweetheart. Since we're gonna date and break up and all."

His smile reappeared. "Why are we going to break up... sweetheart?" Yeah, the endearment fit.

No response. Only a soft snore. He snickered. She'd already fallen asleep, hadn't she?

Conrad didn't dare hang up. As promised, he kept the connection open. But it wasn't long before a wave of peace washed over him. His eyelids grew heavy and...

The next thing Conrad knew, a hacking cough jolted him awake. He blinked, gradually growing alert. And shocked. He'd slept. For the first time in ages, he'd actually slept. Sunlight shone through his bedroom window.

When the coughing ceased, a series of meows started up. "Mommy heard you already, baby. No reason to repeat yourself a third time. I'll—" *Click.*

Not wanting to miss a call—*please be another call*—he kept his phone near the bathroom stall as he showered. At the office, in between interviews and a conversation with the boss, he double and triple checked to make sure the ringer operated at full volume. Just in case. Toward the end of his workday, he set up a meeting with Anthony Miller for the following week (finally), but Jane hadn't called.

For the good of the case, Conrad contacted her.

"—turn this alarm off?" she said in lieu of a greeting.

"Jane, it's Conrad," he began, everything suddenly right in his world. "I need to visit the Garden today to place—"

GENA SHOWALTER & JILL MONROE

"Oh, there's the button," she muttered. "Sleepy night-night time now." *Click.*

Snort. With a crew in tow, Conrad drove to the Garden to set up hidden cameras around Muffin's headstone just in case the murderer returned for the crowbar. He parked beside a truck, sent the agents to the site, and knocked on the door, but Jane never responded. Sleeping too deeply?

"She's dead to the world when the medicine kicks in." The flatly uttered statement came from his right.

Conrad turned to find a shirtless, sweating Beau striding past the porch, hauling a piece of timber. The man's level of aggression hadn't faded, but no matter. Whether Beau liked it or not, Jane saw him as a sibling; he stood no chance with her.

"What are your intentions toward her?" Beau asked as he hefted the wood into the back of his truck.

Conrad arched a brow. "That isn't any of your business, now, is it?"

"I've been hired as her chief security officer. Everything about her safety is my business."

Speaking of her safety, Conrad told him, "She mentioned people are coming out here to examine the crime scene."

"Don't worry. They don't stay for long," Beau assured him. His biceps flexed as he wiped a rag over his face. "I protect her. I'll *always* protect her. I came back to be with her."

Okay, they'd do this here and now. "I don't care what you came back to do. Your intentions won't stop me from doing what I want."

The other man studied him in silence. "You feel it when you look at her, don't you?"

No reason to pretend to misunderstand. "The peace? Yeah. I do."

"Figured." The stiffness left Beau as he heaved a sigh. "You won't take her for granted, at least." That said, he climbed into the truck and drove off.

A concession? With a lighter step, Conrad joined his coworkers at Muffin's headstone.

Jane's next call arrived on the drive back to the office. She said, "You are so sweet, and I miss you so much. Bring me Daisy's soon," then hung up.

After that, she rang him throughout the day, and yes, whenever possible he stopped what he was doing to answer. He met both the rage monster and the diaper baby, as well as the quirky gravekeeper with no filter. His top five favorite Jane-isms, in no particular order:

- "Why, why, why will no one bring me chicken noodle soup? Do they not understand I'm in the process of *dying?*"
- "Oh! Colds are the worst, and I'm just so jazzed. So jazzed! Avenge me, Conrad. No mercy!"
- "You know what's criminal? You in a shirt."
- "Rolex's new name is Pickles Dee Licious. I guess that makes me Sweet Pepper Divine."
- "Bet you ten bazillion dollars I'll solve the case before you do."

Her sleuthing wasn't going to stop. Noted. Perhaps there was a way to involve her in the case without putting her in any danger. If the little history buff knew more about the gold than she realized, she could be a huge help and feel useful while scoring him major points.

Before heading home for the evening, Conrad dropped by Ms. Randall's office. Perfect timing. The receptionist had already left, and the office door was open. He stopped in the frame and knocked.

The older woman glanced up from a file on her desk.

"Tell me you're here with a solve on the Hotchkins case," she demanded, following the question with an impatient wave of her fingers.

"I'm still filling in the pieces. The gold remains a top motive, despite the doctor's legion of lovers. That's the reason I'd like to share certain details with Jane Ladling, the owner of Garden of Memories. Things we've held back from the public."

Ms. Randall lifted a brow before returning her attention to the file. "Explain your logic."

"First, she's not a suspect. Second, we've hit a brick wall with the Order of Seven, the town's rumored secret society. And third, her ancestor was a founding member. As a bonus fourth, her home is considered a burial site for much of the gold."

"So what is it you think she knows?" Ms. Randall leaned back in her chair and joined her fingers over her middle, the file now forgotten.

He gave the only honest answer. "More."

A sigh parted her lips. "Very well. Do it. Let's find out what she knows."

"Thank you, ma'am."

Conrad grinned the entire drive home. As he slipped past his front door, his phone rang. His grin only widened when he spotted the caller's name.

He answered as quickly as humanly possible. "Hello, Jane." Knowing she could hang up at any second without warning, he seized the opportunity to ask a question burning in his mind. "What are your top three dating deal breakers?"

She sneezed. "Um, probably Rolex's disapproval, a name that does or does not start with C and being dead. I'm pretty sure William King in plot 211 strips me with his empty sockets every time I walk by."

So much to unpack here. Rolex's approval, huh?

Then she added, "Be honest. Do you think cereal is a soup?"

"I do not."

"You're probably right. But chicken noodle soup is soup."

He snorted. "Are you hungry for Daisy's, sweetheart?"

"Maybe. It cures everything. Okay bye!"

Hours later, the phone rang again. More than ready, he answered, "I hoped you'd call." Next burning question. "What was your first thought when we met?"

"Probably me-ow."

A meow fit the leering he'd never forgotten.

Suddenly she burst out, "Tell me everything you know about the case immediately or we're finished forever!"

She spoke as if they were already in the middle of a relationship. And he wasn't mad about it. "I'll tell you when you're better."

"If you break my heart," she blurted out next, "I'm going to break your face."

"Thank you for the warning. Listen, sweetheart. I doubt you'll remember this, but I'm telling you anyway. We replaced the crowbar on Muffin's marker with a duplicate. We also hid some cameras in the area, just in case."

A lengthy pause. Not uncommon during these cold medicine-induced phone calls. Then she gasped. "Guess what? You're falling in love with me, but you should stop 'cause I'm cursed."

Him, falling in love? Please. It hadn't happened in thirty-five years. Wasn't happening now. There were too many frayed wires in his heart. But he seized on the information about her. "Cursed, huh? I'm intrigued. Tell me more."

A moment of silence, then a startled thrill. "Wouldn't it be amazing if turtles had wings? They would finally have a higher perspective. Wait. Beau traveled the world with the military, I bet. What if he saw one?" *Click.*

Conrad laughed, but his amusement didn't last long. He might not have the ability to love...but Jane did. And she was the one who'd introduced the emotion to the conversation, indicating the L word had crossed her mind lately. Deep down, did she believe *she* could fall in love with *him*?

He rubbed a fist into a chest suddenly far too tight for his comfort. What would he do if she did?

TWO DAYS LATER, Conrad held a bag filled with food from Daisy's in one hand and knocked on Jane's door with the other. There'd been no calls last night or this morning. She must be feeling better.

Stay away another day? Impossible.

Thankfully, it wasn't long before he detected the patter of light footsteps. His heartbeat picked up speed.

He held his breath as the door swung open... *Punch.* There she was. She wore jeans and a T-shirt, her long hair damp and hanging free. Dark circles created half-moons under her eyes. Shades of pink and red stained her cheeks and the tip of her nose.

Had he ever seen a lovelier creature?

"What?" she demanded, fidgeting. The scent of honeysuckle, roses and magnolia wafted from her. She ran her bottom lip between her teeth. "I mean, what can I help you with, detective?"

Detective? Seriously? A smile attempted to fight its way free. Did she remember any of their conversations? "Oh wonderful," he said. "You didn't threaten to feed me my own organs today. You must feel better. The red nose is a cute touch, though."

Horror flashed in her eyes. "It's pink!"

"And the clothes." He looked her over. Slowly. "And that thousand-dollars-an-hour voice."

Confusion replaced the horror. "That what?"

The grin almost won the battle. Maybe she *didn't* recall their chats. He entered her cottage, the knitted throw that was on the back of the couch now a tangled mess halfway between a cushion and the floor.

Behind him, she squeaked, "I never said I would feed you your own organs. Did I?"

Nope. She didn't remember. And how fortuitous was that? "You most certainly did." Not waiting for her lead, he moved deeper into the home, on the lookout for—here. The kitchen. "Twice," he added, placing items from the bag on a chipped yellow counter.

A peninsula separated the kitchen from a dining area that was dominated by a large table well able to seat a legion at any holiday. A smaller table filled a corner of the kitchen, creating a more intimate space. He could easily imagine having a morning coffee there.

Something he wanted. Badly.

Jane joined him, Rolex not far behind. She gasped. "You went to Daisy's. Her chicken noodle soup is a magic cure-all for everything wrong in everyone's world."

"You told me." He dug deep into the bag. Excellent. Daisy had included two plastic spoons. "A million times."

Eyes wide, she bypassed his comment and asked, "Just to be clear, you brought chicken noodle soup for me? Jane."

"That *is* what you requested, right?"

She pressed her hands to her stomach. "Thank you, Conrad. I'm speechless."

"Don't say that." He winked at her. "I should be rewarded for my good deed, not punished."

Shock crossed over her features as she sank into a

wooden chair on the opposite side of the peninsula. "What else did I ask you to do?"

The cat jumped into the chair at her right, staring at Conrad with murderous schemes in his eyes. *I will win you over.*

"Ask?" He internally snorted. "You demanded I update you on the case. To save my very life, I'm here with information."

He withdrew the sweet bread and set the loaf on a cutting board he found stashed near the stove. "Here's the thing. I'm human, and I'm due a lunch break. Why not eat it here with you and discuss the investigation? Two birds, one stone. All above board. Mostly. I promise I'll tell you as much as I can."

"Yes, please and thank you," she said, stretching out her arms and waving her fingers, demanding the soup.

He didn't think there was anything better than conversing with this cupcake of a human. "Hungry?"

"Starved. I didn't know it until this moment."

Satisfaction overtook him. Maybe his DNA had ancient ties to the cavemaniest cavemen ever to walk the Earth, because he liked meeting her needs.

Clink, clink, clink. The sound of metal hitting metal reached his ears. Then pounding footsteps. Then the slam of a car door. Well. Beau was letting him know he was on the scene, ready to come to Jane's rescue if necessary. Good man. Conrad couldn't help but admire his fortitude.

"Butter?" he asked Jane.

She jolted, as if startled from faraway thoughts, her gaze zooming to him, then the bread. A slight smile bloomed. "Yes, please. Like Daisy's soup, butter makes everything better."

His next words slipped out unbidden. "I'm beginning to believe there are people who make everything better too. What do you think?"

"Um." Her eyes widened as she squirmed in her seat. "Maybe?"

He wasn't sure he'd ever left someone better than he'd found them...but he suddenly wanted to.

Dead body. Beautiful brunette. He stalked over and plopped into the chair to Jane's left. "The case." His gift to her. "We're pursuing a couple different leads and motives and questioning several people of interest." Information he'd given her before.

"Oh?" A casual tone belied a sparkle of excitement. She propped her elbows on the countertop, peering over at him, seeming totally absorbed in him. She looked like every dream he'd ever had and even some he hadn't. "Tell me more."

She was a real-life fairytale princess, wasn't she?

Needing a moment, he added more butter to his bread. "The doctor had an active sex life outside of his marriage. Many of those women had a boyfriend or husband. On the other hand, we found evidence to indicate the doctor had recently developed a passion for hunting treasure."

"So the motive is love or money," she replied, thoughtful.

"The motive is always love or money. One or the other."

Her brow scrunched up. "I don't understand what either has to do with the cemetery, though. I mean, a graveyard rarely evokes feelings of romance or greed."

"You'd be surprised." Since discovering this particular cemetery, he'd entertained more romantic thoughts than...ever.

"And treasure?" she continued, stirring her soup. She blew on the surface. "Everyone knows the cemetery was once raided and stripped of any hidden gold. Unless new rumors surfaced?"

Not widely. Not yet. "Has anyone mentioned a connection between the fleur-de-lys that's been showing up around town and the legends about the gold?"

She stared off into space while chewing on her bottom lip, reminding him of the moment they'd met. Flipping through her mental files? Wilting with disappointment, she said, "No. They haven't."

Too bad. He could have asked something about the Order of Seven. He nudged her shoulder with his own instead, determined to cheer her up. "C'mon. Finish your soup, and I'll show you what I ordered for dessert."

She grinned, thrilling him. Diving into her soup, she closed her eyes and moaned. Then she stiffened, froze and frowned. "Why are you being so nice to me, Special Agent Conrad Ryan?"

Voice throaty, he asked, "Am I usually cruel to you?"

"You're usually closed off. Which is cruel to someone like me. So yes. You are usually cruel to me."

I will kiss it and make it better. "Let's say my job leaves me unnaturally suspicious of everyone I meet. The actions they take. The words they use. Having a traumatic childhood doesn't help matters." But none of those things had guarded him from her appeal.

Sympathy welled in her eyes, and it was almost more than he could withstand. "Conrad—"

"Nope." That soft tone of hers! Worse than those glorious baby blues. "I'm done." No more personal stuff today. He anchored the lid on his soup, an outward version of his inward shutdown.

The sympathy only deepened. He should go. He—lost his train of thought. Appearing a bit dazed, she reached out and traced her fingertips over the tattoos on his forearm.

His muscles jumped and tingled. He wanted to reach back. Not following the urge required a resolve he didn't think he could maintain for long. Better to move on —for now.

He adjusted his position, ending the contact. "Ready for that dessert?"

A blush stained her cheeks as he withdrew peanut butter cookies from the bag. In an act of mercy, she allowed the subject to change and snatched the biggest from his clasp, complaining, "It's as if you can read my mind."

How he liked this woman. "I think I can do anything but that. Reading you is tough. You show too much and too little at the same time. I've never struggled to read anyone like this."

A tinkling laugh escaped her, and his gut tightened. There it was; his addiction. Before she had a chance to respond to his words, a knock sounded at the back door. She gasped, startling again.

"Beau," he said, brow arched.

"Hopefully." Nibbling on the cookie, she hopped up and strolled to the door.

Conrad rose as well and trailed her but stopped several feet back to lean a shoulder against a wall.

Beau occupied the other side of the entrance. His discomfort was clear as he balanced a small plastic, lidded bowl in his hands.

"Hi," she said, and Conrad had no problem seeing the truth now. She'd meant what she'd said. Zero romantic interest in Beau. She projected all kinds of warmth, but no real heat. There wasn't a blip of a leer. "Please, come in."

"No, thank you." His gaze slid to Conrad to pass a message. *I concede. I'm trusting you with her. For now.* "I saw his car and thought you might need support."

What a great day this had turned out to be.

Jane offered her friend a sweet smile. "That's so kind, but I'm great. Conrad brought my favorite soup. We've been

79

conferring about the case." The delighted pride in her tone... yeah, it did something to him.

"How are you feeling?" Beau asked, being respectful of her choice. "Truly?"

"Good enough to remember our deal. Don't think you're getting out of it. Oh! While I've got you, we need to discuss the bill you haven't given me."

The other man stepped backward and shook his head. "Just haven't gotten around to it yet."

"Beau, I insist on paying you. And don't forget to put your sign at the gate. If you haven't already." She motioned to the kitchen. "Are you sure you don't want to come in? We can brainstorm the coming date—"

Beau flinched ever so slightly. "This is for you." He thrust the container her way. "I brought you soup as well."

She brightened. "Thank you, Beau. I love it."

The vet deadpanned, "You haven't even tasted it. It's not from Daisy's." He grew visibly embarrassed. "I, uh, made it. On my own."

Conrad winced at the other man. Rookie mistake. Always give the woman what she wants.

"It smells delicious," she said, "and now I have dinner. So about that deal. You're keeping your end of the bargain, yes?"

Wait. Bargain? What bargain?

"I'll call you about the date, okay?" Beau spun on his heel and took off.

"I consider that a definite yes," she called, before shutting the door.

"Date?" Conrad closed the distance, determined to unearth an answer. His hands curled into fists.

She faced him, giving a start at his nearness. "A double." Gazing up at him through the thick fan of her lashes, she said, "Hey, speaking of, do you happen to know a single man who might be willing to have dinner with me? Unless this is considered a conflict of interest?"

Had she just asked him out? "I'm still confused. Double date?"

"I'm setting Beau up with this really great girl, possibly, but he insists I bring a date too. Therefore, I'm on the prowl."

"He insists," Conrad echoed, caught up in his question. Had she asked him out or not?

"I think he's shy," she continued, "and I'm a safety net. Everyone needs a support system."

"I get that." If she hadn't invited Conrad to a romantic evening, she'd hinted about a set up with someone he knew. "Why do you want to meet one of my friends?" he asked, in case that was her meaning.

She spun with dramatic flair and pressed against the counter. "No one in town is interested in me and that's okay, because I'm not interested in any of them either. Truth be told, I'm pretty anti-relationships."

That...hmm. That wasn't what he'd expected to hear. Even though she'd once told him she would never fall in love or marry. "Explain."

"I'm a victim of the Ladling curse, and that's all I'm willing to say."

She'd mentioned the curse before, when she'd been high on cold medicine. He'd been intrigued then, and he was intrigued now. He closed the distance once again. Light bounced off her dark hair, distracting him from his objective, and he paused to pinch a soft lock.

Concentrate. "One day soon, we'll dissect this curse together. I want every detail, and you'll give them to me. But I won't be introducing you to my friends, Jane." Not that he had any. "When you go on that double date with Beau, I will be at your side. Me." He'd admitted too much. He didn't care.

GENA SHOWALTER & JILL MONROE

Better to make clear his intentions and stake his claim while he had the chance.

She shivered against him.

Liked what he'd had to say? Good. He bent down, putting his mouth to her ear. "Goodnight, sweetheart."

Get this case solved and get the girl.

CHAPTER SEVEN

Your tattoos tell a story. If your particular tale is a heart-
wrencher, expect a hug
–A Gravekeeper's Guide to Dating

Conrad eyed the man across the table. Anthony "Tony" Miller, an attorney at Hagger, Hagger and Miller. A firm known to cater to the wealthiest members of Aurelian Hills. Mr. Miller was also a suspicious spouse who'd shown up at GBH HQ half an hour late for an agreed upon interview.

An agitated man with salt and pepper hair whose age appeared to be anywhere between fifty and seventy-five. The consequence of his hard, fast living, stress, or the guilt of committing murder? A jumble of emotion filled bloodshot eyes framed by deep lines. A dark stain marred his wrinkled shirt. He reeked of gas station cologne and cigarette smoke. Shaky hands suggested either too much alcohol or too little.

"Well?" the guy demanded, already belligerent.

Capable of plotting a homicide? Certainly. Might as well dig in. "Did you kill Marcus Hotchkins?"

Smug all of a sudden, he leaned back in his chair and crossed his arms. "No. Next question."

"Did you ever hunt gold with him?"

"No. Next."

Accomplished liar or eager truth teller? "The night of the murder, you left your house angry and issuing threats. You didn't return home until the next morning."

"Yes, and nothing you mentioned is illegal. I drove to Atlanta, got a room at the Ritz and visited the bar. Spent the night with a sexy blond. We didn't exchange names, if you know what I mean, but I'm sure the bartender can verify my presence. Next."

Looked like Conrad would be sending agents to the Ritz. "Did you pay for your room or the drinks with a credit card?"

The smugness returned. "No. I paid in cash, using the money Em saved, and thought she'd hidden from me. Next."

Okay. Time to switch gears. "You believed Dr. Hotchkins was sleeping with your wife, yes?"

"Yes, but only because he was. I didn't kill him, though. I wanted him to live so I could gather irrefutable evidence and present it to his wife. Blowing up his marriage was my right."

"Did you send anonymous texts to Tiffany Miller, alerting her to the doctor's affair with a patient?" Had Mr. Miller known of his wife and her boss before the night of the murder?

"Can you prove I sent her any texts?"

So, yes.

"I wanted him alive for years to come, giving me the opportunity to destroy his world piece by piece." Scowling, Miller spread his arms. "What do I have to live for now?"

All right, what was with the people of Aurelian Hills and revenge? Was there something in the water? At least the attorney wasn't faking ignorance. "Stealing his gold while he lived and spending it after he died isn't revenge enough?"

"Are you saying Marcus Hotchkins actually found gold?" the other man demanded. The unearned arrogance faded. "At the cemetery?"

Genuinely surprised? Conrad ignored the questions and asked another. "What makes you so certain your wife and the doctor were having an affair?"

"Someone mailed me a note," the attorney groused, seeming to forget the gold as he recalled his anger. "Said they saw her kissing him at the clinic in Atlanta where they both volunteered. Summerhill Community Pediatric."

A lead worth following. "You believed this report without solid proof?"

"Not at first." Miller's fingers flexed, as if he were holding an unseen cup. "I followed her, watched her interact with him outside a sleazy motel. If you could have seen the sparks between them."

"Sparks aren't exactly proof that will hold up in court." Something a defensive attorney would mention.

Invisible thorns of hostility flared over his skin. "They are when I'm the judge and jury."

"And the executioner?"

Miller slitted his eyelids and stood, the chair legs scraping across the floor. "And now we're done here."

Yes, they were. Until Conrad checked the veracity of the man's alibi, he had no other questions.

Miller exited the room and Hightower entered. She met Conrad's gaze. "I've been monitoring a growing thread on the Headliner that concretely links the rumors about gold to the Garden of Memories. More and more people are suspecting your groundskeeper of hoarding nuggets."

Suggesting Jane could be in danger. He scrubbed a hand down his face.

"Also," she continued, "I confirmed Dr. Hotchkins bought a car last month. He answered an ad in the paper and paid cash. There's evidence to indicate he stored it outside his neighborhood. Problem is, it's not there, and local law enforcement hasn't picked up any abandoned vehicles in town. I bet he drove it the night of his murder and hid it somewhere near the cemetery."

This. This could be the break they needed. If the doctor gave his partner a ride, there could be prints inside the vehicle. "Find it," he commanded. "Take a team and scour every inch of land."

FROTHING WITH DETERMINATION, Conrad approached Summerhill Community Pediatric with Barrow at his side. A large metal building shaped like a barn showcased a wall of windows and a wraparound porch. Rose bushes and peach trees added another level of southern charm, a sight he might have appreciated at any other time. Here, now, he cared only about solving the case.

Inside the sunlit building, a crowd gathered to celebrate the life of Dr. Hotchkins. The very reason Conrad chose this day and time to visit. Everyone he wanted to interview congregated under one roof.

Bouquets of flowers abounded, most arrayed behind a long table scattered with personal and professional pictures of Dr. Hotchkins. Another table offered a smorgasbord of snacks.

At low volume, he told his partner, "Take pictures of the photos without being obvious."

"Will do." Barrow broke from him to comply.

CONRAD: FALLING FOR THE GRAVEKEEPER

Conrad scanned the sea of faces for Dr. Diana Holmgren. According to the company website, she was in charge of scheduling the volunteers. There. The forty-three-year-old general practitioner sipped something clear from a glass and spoke with a group of people, looking exactly as she did on the site's personnel page. Stern and tidy.

He strode over, introduced himself and flashed his badge, then ushered Dr. Holmgren aside for a chat. Diving right in, he asked, "Did Dr. Hotchkins ever bring someone with him when he volunteered here?"

"Emma Miller and Caroline Whittington. Why?" She flattened her palm beneath her collarbone. "Do you think one of them might be the killer?"

"I can neither confirm nor deny that." He mashed his lips to cut off a sigh when her eyes lit with suspicion. Serving up the standard line always invited more speculation. "How often did he bring them?"

"Most times he came with Emma. Only sometimes did he bring Caroline. Once, he brought both. Why?" she repeated.

He side-stepped the query, asking, "Did you notice any signs of a romantic relationship with either woman?"

Her brows drew together. "I have no desire to speak ill of the dead, but for the sake of justice, I will share what I know." She dragged in a deep breath. "I think he and Emma had something going on the side. I only saw them making eyes at each other but another volunteer believes he spotted them kissing in a car. Plus, Dr. Hotchkins tended to be extra handsy with Emma, always patting her shoulder in a job well done. And she wasn't uncomfortable with the attention, either. Caroline, though, I'm not sure. He never patted her, but he may have called her muffin once."

A romantic food nickname? A slip of the tongue? An innocent request for a snack? A reference to the cemetery's guard dog? Something else to add to his growing list of tasks:

87

Speak with Ms. Whittington again. Mrs. Miller had some explaining to do, too. The deeper he dug, the more her motive for murder expanded and solidified.

"There's something else," the general practitioner piped up. "Not too long ago, Emma's husband stormed inside and slugged Dr. Hotchkins in the face."

Hmm. No complaint had been filed, or Conrad would have found it. So. Anthony Miller had a violent temper, as suspected. "Did either man mention anything about gold, treasure or nuggets?"

She thought for a moment, then shook her head. "No, I don't think so."

His cell phone buzzed, signaling a text. He checked the screen.

> Hightower: Dr. Hotchkins's second car was hidden near the cemetery and wiped clean of evidence. We don't think he drove with a companion, though. There's an additional set of tire tracks to suggest they met.

> Conrad: Do we know the make and model of the second car yet?

> Hightower: Nothing so far. Techs think the pattern will be too difficult to properly identify.

He huffed a breath.

"Anything else, agent?" Holmgren asked, a bit impatient.

He pulled from his thoughts and prepared to respond, but the front door of the building swung back, allowing a brighter beam of light inside—Jane appeared in the center of it, and the words died on his tongue.

Punch. Conrad's mind blanked. She wore a tight black dress that conformed to her curves. Hair like rich brown silk curled more than usual. She'd pinned back the sides. Beau towered behind her, clearly uncomfortable in a white button down and slacks.

Wide eyed, the beautiful gravekeeper who believed in mysterious curses peered around the lobby—her jaw slackened when she spotted Conrad.

His synapsis started firing again, and he arched a brow at her. Caught her investigating red handed. But it wasn't anger or worry he experienced. Oh no. He was a starving man who'd just discovered an all you can eat banquet.

"Agent?" Dr. Holmgren prompted.

He forced himself to look away from Jane, to pretend he was back to business as usual. He refocused on the doctor in front of him, but kept the brunette in his periphery. "I have one more question for you."

Beau bent his head to say something to Jane. Whatever it was thrilled her. A smile, somehow both innocent and calculated, bloomed over her face, and the two broke apart, heading in separate directions. *She plans to play a game of cat and mouse with me.*

Bring it. This cat had rabies.

"Excuse me," he muttered. He trailed Jane to the hors d'oeuvres table but circled her rather than approach as she twice sampled something from every dish. Had she forgotten her mission already?

Ready to strike, Conrad moved in. Midway, Beau stepped into his path. As expected.

"Just let her have her fun," the other man griped. "She's not hurting anything."

"I will never put her amusement before her life. Right now, a murderer who traipsed all over her property remains at large."

"She isn't in any danger when I'm there," the vet bragged, and Conrad believed him.

Still. "Don't be a child, Harden. You can't be there all the time, nor can you control everything."

The other man snorted, offering his first show of humor. "Neither can you, Ryan. Not when that everything is Jane Ladling." With the semblance of a smile, he walked away.

Surveilling Jane once she finished snacking was easy. She made several sweeps around the room, inserting herself into conversations and—nope, not finished snacking, after all. She pilfered food from the snack table between visiting with guests. Approaching her, however, proved impossible. Anytime he attempted to close in, Beau interfered.

When Conrad spotted his prey, err, protectee, chatting with people signing a guest book, he aimed straight for her. No sign of the–nope. Spoke too soon. Beau planted himself in Conrad's path.

"Nice weather," the other man offered.

Conrad ditched him and awaited another opportunity to strike. As Jane conversed with a group standing near a long table that displayed pictures of the doctor and some of the children he'd saved, Conrad braced to move in.

Beau shoved a cup of punch his way. "Thirsty?"

With a growl, Conrad broke from the vet to reassess his strategy. It was ten minutes later, as Jane lingered near a trash can, waiting for various mourners to throw away their buffet plates, that he got close enough to overhear the same conversation she overheard. Her eyes lit up at the mention of Anthony Miller.

Miss Amateur Sleuth had just found her next clue.

Her day had gotten better while Conrad's only grew worse. A weight settled hard in his stomach. He did not want her going near Mr. Miller.

Okay, time to get serious about stopping her. No more encouragement. Conrad crossed to Barrow. "Distract Miss Ladling's companion. The muscular blond."

"Consider it done." The other agent hastened off.

The second Barrow cornered Beau, Conrad marched to Jane. The former soldier noticed, of course, and rudely abandoned Barrow to rush up behind his charge and sound the alarm. Straightening, she spun in Conrad's direction. Multiple finger sandwiches filled her hands. Nervous excitement flittered over her features.

"What are you doing here, Jane?" he demanded, doing his best to ignore her incredible scent and the undeniable charm of her. Oh, he knew why she was here. He wanted her to admit the words aloud.

"Don't answer that," Beau interjected.

Conrad glared at him, projecting a message. *You suck, man.*

The vet projected a smug reply. *I know.*

Jane glanced between them before focusing those sparkling blues on Conrad. She was loving this. She even stuffed a sandwich in her mouth to buy time. If she made him smile right now, he would be so ticked. At least he had the presence of mind to hold his tongue. He refused to break first.

She gulped, finally rasping, "Am I committing a crime, officer?"

"It's detective—" Okay, it was official. She had scrambled his brain. "It's special agent. And you tell me. *Are* you committing a crime?"

"No?" A question rather than a statement. But in a snap of time, her hesitation morphed into unshakable determination. "I'm performing a public service. In fact, I already have a lead in our case."

"My case. Mine." He slid into her personal space, bringing his own determination to the table. He wouldn't lose this negotiation. Not when her safety factored into the equation. "You will not follow this lead, Jane. Say it. Let me hear you."

Shoulders rolling in, she peered at him through long, curling lashes. Her heart-shaped mouth tilted in an adorable pout. "But you haven't even heard my idea yet."

Those eyes. That look. How was he supposed to win anything ever? *Stay strong.* "I don't need an explanation. I can guess. You suspect Emma Miller's husband, and you're planning to question him. But you won't do it because I'm telling you not to. You will not visit his office, and you most definitely will not show up on his doorstep. I mean it, Jane."

Her stubborn side rallied, beaming pure obstinance at him. "Not a bad deduction, Officer Detective Special Agent Conrad Ryan."

No retreat, no surrender. "Jane," he said, pushing her name past gritted teeth. Conrad's last stand. If this didn't work...

"Oh, all right," she burst out. "Fine. You win, okay? I won't drop by Mr. Miller's office or show up on his doorstep."

Wait. What? Conrad had actually won this round?

"Now, if you'll excuse us." Nose in the air, she eased backward, bumping into Beau. She would have fallen if the vet hadn't caught her. For some reason, she refused to meet Conrad's gaze again.

Oh, no, no, no. He'd somehow lost, hadn't he? "Jane." Talk about a premature celebration. The woman clearly expected to speak with Miller in a way Conrad hadn't considered.

"Nope, no need to continue saying what you're saying," she said with a humph. "Trust me. I've already deduced the highlights. You meant every word. I'll be in huge trouble if I disobey. And finally, I better go home and stay there or else." She spread her arms, all haughty disdain. "See? I can detective like a boss, too."

So he needed a different mode of attack. Noted. "And if the killer decides to go after *you?*" If anyone dared to hurt her... His hands curled into fists. *I might be the one going to jail.*

"There's no stronger motivation to catch the fiend as quickly as possible," she said, even haughtier.

Obviously, there would be no stopping her. Desperate, he looked to Beau. "You'll keep her safe."

"I will." Beau nodded. "I'll take a bullet for her if necessary."

That, Conrad believed. And suddenly, he more than liked the guy. He was grateful for his presence in her life.

"No one is taking a bullet for anyone," Jane rushed out, morphing into a prim schoolteacher chiding misbehaving children.

Conrad pressed his tongue to the roof of his mouth, torn between telling her to go home and enfolding her against him to prevent her from going anywhere else.

Beau tugged her toward the door, drawing her away. Conrad couldn't pull his gaze from her. Didn't want to. Because she didn't pull her gaze from him. She offered him a little wave before she vanished beyond the door.

Falling for her?

He just might be.

CHAPTER EIGHT

Unwavering confidence will get you far in life. Especially if you want to date gravekeepers who believe they're cursed in love.

–A Gravekeeper's Guide to Dating

*C*onrad tossed and turned for hours. A thousand times, he almost picked up his phone and rang Jane. How quickly he'd grown used to their under-the-influence-of-cold-medicine conversations. Maybe, if he heard her voice, he could drift to sleep and awake refreshed again. But he shouldn't do it. A midnight call? Far from professional. What if he woke her?

Yes, but what if he didn't wake her? What if she wasn't sleeping, either, because she hoped to hear from him?

Finally he allowed temptation to get the better of him and swiped up his phone. Just before he keyed up her number, however, he noticed an email from Hightower regarding Anthony Miller.

Conrad jolted upright, his lips pursing as he read the message. *Miller's alibi checks out. A bartender verified his pres-*

ence at the hotel bar and even identified the woman he took to his room. A working girl. She's there every night. Her shift starts at 9. I stopped by and spoke with her, and she told me Miller paid for the entire evening.

So. The lawyer was a scumbag, but he wasn't the killer. A true shocker. Conrad would have put money on Mr. Miller's guilt.

Who did that leave? Miller's wife, who'd lied to authorities. She'd absolutely had an affair with her boss. Perhaps she'd thought she was the only one Hotchkins had loved, learned otherwise, and snapped?

And what of Dr. Garcia, who might have helped in an attempt to save the clinic?

Or Whittington, who might or might not be nicknamed Muffin?

Of course, there was also the embittered widow, jealous significant others, and the mysterious gold hunter, who could be any of the aforementioned people.

There'd been no clues to unearth his or her identity. But. The day of his murder, as well as a string of other days, Hotchkins had drawn three chili peppers near a swirling circle in his planner. In the beginning, everyone had assumed the two images were separate—the spicy grading system and a symbol for a lover. But what if they belonged together? A type of fleur-de-lys?

Look at the large number of vehicles tagged with the fleur-de-lys graffiti. In some way or another, many of the owners were involved in the case. Some were even mentioned in Hotchkins's planner. Those the GBH had decoded, anyway. Over half graced the list of lovers that Whittington and Garcia put together.

There had to be a connection.

Conrad's phone vibrated, drawing his attention. A text from Beau.

> B. Harden: FYI. We spoke with Miller at a bar. Before you complain, don't. This was needed. Now he knows someone is watching Jane's back.

Beau needed to learn to tell the beautiful brunette no.

A subtle shakiness invaded Conrad's limbs. He typed, *If you want to keep something, you do what's best for it even when it hurts.*

> B. Harden: What does that even mean? And what are you still doing up?

> Conrad: What are YOU doing up?

Two could play this game. Don't ask what you don't want to answer.

> B. Harden: Moving on. What will you do if she solves the case first?????

> Conrad: I don't know. Probably marry her.

He meant the words as a joke. Of course he did. There was zero reason to ponder anything else about the matter.

As minutes passed without a new text, he fell back on his pillows and scrubbed a hand over his face. He and Jane would have a sit down tomorrow. He'd explain how things must go from here on out, and she would fall into line. And that was just how it was gonna be.

Should I pound my chest now or later?

He snorted. Jane Ladling might require a bit more finesse on his part. Might? Ha! But he learned, and he adapted.

Eager to begin, he rose with the sun, showered, and dressed, then drove to the GBH headquarters, taking back roads to bypass traffic. After speaking with Ms. Randall, he shut himself in his office and plopped into the chair at his desk. Already brimming with satisfaction, he keyed up Jane's number.

"Why, Special Agent Conrad Ryan," she cooed upon answering. "As I live and breathe."

The sugary sweetness of her voice broadcasted a thousand watts of sass. His timbre dipped of its own accord. "Is raising my blood pressure a new game you're playing?"

She gasped with genuine astonishment. "Wait. You know about Tony, don't you? How?"

"I have eyes and ears everywhere," he told her with a wry tone.

"Did Beau tell you? He did, didn't he?"

"The tattletale doesn't matter. You're visiting me at my office today. Two hours. Don't argue. I'll text you the address. Don't be late, either." Okay, so, he lacked finesse of any kind.

"A tour? For me?" she squealed with so much happiness he felt as if a sun dawned inside his chest.

"See you soon, Jane." *Click.* Instant regret. He missed her voice. But so what. He had a lesson to teach.

Waiting two hours for her arrival—one hundred and twenty endless minutes—proved excruciating. He survived only by focusing on his main objective: solving the case. Conrad dissected statements he'd already dissected, hoping to glean something new.

Twenty-seven seconds before his internal timer went off, he noticed a pacing shadow through the crack under his door. Jane, thinking about running?

Amusement mingled with relief. "Are you planning to stand outside or come in?" he called.

"I'm debating," she called back. Moments later, the knob turned. With her head high, she strolled into the room wearing a shorter-than-usual dress of black-and-white. Dark hair fell loose and curling, with a small hat pinned to her crown. Her baby blues glittered. A blush already painted her cheeks.

Punch. He struggled to maintain a stern expression. "Sit," he commanded, motioning to a chair in front of his desk. *Safety first.*

She scrunched her nose, as if she didn't understand his language. "What about the tour?"

Did she have any sense of self-preservation? Well, outside of the supposed curse. Which she had never fully explained. "There won't be a tour." He used his flattest tone to let her know he meant business.

Instant disappointment radiated from her. "But I want to see the crime lab."

"Then you should have gone home after the memorial service." How he resisted the urge to give in, he might never know. "GBH tours are only offered to well-behaved murder suspects."

"Guess that means the cybersecurity unit is out too," she grumbled. Dragging her feet, she moved to the chair he'd suggested and plopped down. "Am I here so you can scare me straight?"

"Someone needs to." There wasn't an ounce of remorse in her demeanor. "You have no business following leads. You'll only go down the wrong roads because you aren't privy to all the facts."

"You're right. I'm not privy to all the facts. And I think we can both agree that is one hundred percent your fault." She humphed in accusation. "But I'm from the town, and I know the people. I'm a resource. Why aren't you making use of me? Think about it. You're a straight line, and I'm a squiggly one. More creative. I can help you see things from a different perspective."

That, he believed. "Like the flying turtles." *What are you doing? Softening?* Maybe? He formed a steeple with his fingers in front of his mouth, doing his best to look as reserved as possible. "Go on. Elaborate."

Excited, she scooted to the edge of her seat. "Well, I've already worked up multiple motives for multiple people. I'm sorry to say I've just thought of one for you. And it checks out. Solidly. The logic is bulletproof."

The charm of this woman... "Please. Do tell."

"Picture this." As if she were on a stage, speaking to a large audience, she waved her hands and announced, "Weeks before the murder, you passed through my town, spotted me, and instantly became obsessed with me."

So far, her story was plausible.

"You would have settled for any excuse to spend time with me," she continued, clearly warming up to the tale. "When you couldn't think of one, you supplied one with murder."

There was no stopping a burst of amusement. He fought a grin, determined not to encourage this kind of behavior. He'd only be asking for trouble later.

"Your bulletproof logic has a hole," he said, and she braced, as if expecting a blow. "The day we met is the first I'd heard of your town."

The tension drained from her. "So you say. We both know murderers can be liars, too. But okay. Let's pretend you're telling the truth. That just means you saw my picture online and hired an assassin to provide the alibi." She gifted him with the coyest smile. "Though I notice you aren't disputing your attraction to me."

"I don't think anyone can dispute my attraction to you, Jane," he intoned, and her breath hitched. "You'll be pleased to know I gained permission to share other case details with you. But I won't be doing so until you agree to stop speaking with people of interest." He opened his desk drawer and lifted a stack of photos. As her eyes lit, he offered the bounty of visual evidence. "Consider the acceptance of these your agreement." Bribery. His new plan.

More and more excitement emanated from her as she studied the images. "Wait. The fleur-de-lys. Do you think it's a decoy meant to distract from the murder? That Dr. Hotchkins was truly hunting for gold at my cemetery?"

"It's a possibility." More than a possibility. Needing... something, he stood, moved around the desk, and claimed the chair next to hers. Yes. Better. He leaned closer, ridiculously thrilled when he pointed to a photo of plot 39 and their shoulders rubbed together. "Burgundy's coffin was suspected of holding gold bricks and raided. She's mentioned at the exhibit. So are several of your other residents. Maybe the doctor believed a stash of gold was overlooked during the raid."

She turned pensive before shaking her head. "Like I told you, that rumor has surfaced in the past, but longtime citizens know it's false. Dr. Hotchkins is—was—a longtime citizen."

Maybe the people of Aurelian Hills considered the rumor false, maybe not. "We believe he met up with a mistress the night of his murder." Or a partner. Or both. "But we don't know which one, only that she was a regular dish—his words, not mine. He tracked those regulars with a coded calendar. We've identified some but not all."

Her nose wrinkled. "How many, um, regular dishes are there?"

"Eight. With an assortment of semiregulars and one-night stands mixed in. From what we've pieced together, he used the exam rooms as five-minute motels."

Jane cringed. No, this woman had no business being on Whittington's list.

"Was Emma Miller one of the known regulars?" she asked. "Because they were definitely having an affair."

"Yes. But her alibi checked out." Kind of. Mostly. He couldn't get over the fact that she'd lied about the affair. "And so did her husband's." Solidly. Unfortunately.

Jane's pensive air returned, quickly tapering into another bout of excitement. "Give me a chance to study the unknowns in Dr. Hotchkins's code. If his identifiers reflect traits about the women, I'll recognize—"

"No. I'm sorry, but that's out of the question." While seeing what her one-of-a-kind mind did with the symbols intrigued him, he knew Ms. Randall would never approve. Even now, he walked a fine line with what he shared, giving to get while fishing for info, but he never bent or broke the law or divulged too much.

She gaped at him. "You think I might be a member of his rotation? I assure you, I'm not. The doctor wasn't my type. Which is unwaveringly single."

Conrad's top qualification as well. "Until we've successfully identified everyone, I'm not allowed to fully rule anyone out."

"Why are you sharing any case details with me, then, if I'm still a suspect?" she asked, studying him more closely.

His phone rang, but he ignored it to tell her, "I know how it feels for questions to claw at your mind. I swear I will figure this out. You'll have your answers. Just give me time. And peace. I'll work faster—better—if I'm not always worried about you."

Uh-oh. Pure stubbornness etched itself into each of her features. "I have a better idea." Chin up, she stood–the epitome of *bless your heart*. "You learn how to do deep-breathing exercises to control your fear for my well-being, and I'll continue to aid you." She flashed a smile sweeter than honey. Nope, nothing natural here. That grin was one hundred percent artificial. "Thanks for the nontour, Special Agent Ryan. Let's not do it again real soon." Then she was gone.

Conrad remained in his seat, tempted to laugh. Hurricane Jane had struck again. She'd also given him an idea for the case. He reached for the phone to make a call…

CHAPTER NINE

A gruff demeanor can be super cute, if said gruffness comes
with a side of smolder.
–A Gravekeeper's Guide to Dating

*A*n hour later, Conrad hadn't fully recovered from his
interaction with Jane. But recover he must, considering Ms. Randall had scheduled an impromptu Sunday
briefing.

Notebook in hand, he knocked on her office door.

"Come in," she called, tossing her glasses aside as he
entered. "Was the subpoena for the personal electronics of
Hotchkins's coworkers approved?"

"Not yet." He sat in one of two extremely uncomfortable
armchairs in front of a desk covered with files, reports, and
photos of at least ten different cases. How she kept track of
anything with so much chaos, he'd never know. And there
was no way she hadn't chosen these punishing chairs on
purpose. The message was clear: say what needs saying and
get out.

"I'll do what I can to speed the paperwork along." She

leaned back in a softly cushioned and ergonomic chair, all but taunting him. "Did the cemetery owner give us anything good at your meeting?"

"She did." A smile. Internal laughter. An unforgettable farewell. And yes, the idea. "She mentioned longtime citizens of Aurelian Hills know there's no gold buried in the cemetery, which made me think someone new to town might believe the rumors are current and accurate."

"Anyone fit the bill?" Ms. Randall wrinkled her brow.

"The physician assistant, Caroline Whittington, has only lived there a year." A fact that showed up in the preliminary background check performed on every person of interest. "Before that, she spent time in California and Colorado." For schooling, yes, but also for gold? Both states experienced their own gold rush. "On the other hand, Whittington gave us the planner, and she isn't the one who visited the local library to check out books about the town's gold rush. That would be Emma Miller and Abigail Waynes-Kirkland." Jane mentioned each name in the beginning. Mrs. Miller had denied any knowledge of Hotchkins's treasure hunt. But what would Waynes-Kirkland say? "They're friends with the widow but also listed among the doctor's long term mistresses."

"People can forget a rumor is false if they're hoping it's true," Ms. Randall muttered. Tapping the end of a pen against a folder on her desk, she gave a firm nod. "Go back. Speak with his coworkers again. Re-interview the widow. Set a meeting with Waynes-Kirkland. Someone knows something."

"Agreed."

She swiped her readers from the desk and plopped them on her nose. He'd been dismissed. Conrad stood and headed for his office. His phone rang as he crossed the door's threshold. He withdrew the device from his pocket and checked the screen.

Grinning, he eased into his chair and answered. "Calling to make sure I'm doing those deep breathing exercises, Jane?"

"A woman broke into my house while I was gone," she burst out in a panic. "She had a key, Conrad. My brave Rolex chased her out the door, but now he's missing. Fiona is searching the property, and I'm headed to the old office but if I can't find him I'm going to burn the world down and dance in the flames."

Her panic proved contagious, ripping his calm to shreds. He couldn't think past the break in. "Jane! Focus on me." Had the killer come back to destroy evidence left behind? Or eliminate the gravekeeper who might know more than she realized? "Are you hurt?"

"Are you kidding? I'm *dying*, Conrad. My baby is missing."

His chest squeezed. "I meant physically, sweetheart. How are you physically? Are you bleeding?"

"Yes! I'm bleeding internally. My heart is torn into a thousand pieces, and it's more than I can bear."

The squeezing worsened. "We'll figure this out, I swear," he said, grabbing his keys and jetting into the hall. He accidentally bumped into someone but kept going. "I promise I'll stop at nothing to find your baby. But I do need you to stop what you're doing right now and listen to me. I'm on my way to you, but I'm an hour—half an hour out." The sedan had police lights. "Return to your house, bar the door, and dial Beau's number on the landline. He's nearby, and he can reach you faster. Do you understand? Keep me on the cell and tell me every time you complete one of your tasks."

"Oh my gosh! Yes! You're right." A measure of composure entered her voice. "Beau is close, so he can help the search. Thank you, Conrad. Bye." *Click.*

No she did not. He ground his molars. What he didn't do?

Call her back. He reached the parking garage and climbed into his sedan. Lights flashing red and blue, he sped onto the street. He was flying down the highway when Jane's second call came in.

Jabbing the correct button on the console, he opened the line.

"I found him!" she rushed out, unleashing a tide of relief inside Conrad. "I crested a hill, and there he was. Near the old business center. I bet he was searching for me." Her tone hardened. "I will find the woman who did this, and I will *do things*. Don't think I won't. I recorded her on the security feed. She's as good as mine."

Wrong. *As good as mine.* "I want a look at that camera feed. While I'm there, I'll change the locks on your doors. If I leave without losing my mind," he grumbled, "it'll be a miracle." He hung up before he said anything else he shouldn't, not giving her a chance to respond.

Once in town, he stopped at a hardware store to buy everything he needed. When he reached the cottage, he parked beside Beau's truck and emerged. Jane stepped on the porch, a tray of food in hand. She wore a white dress with multi-colored polka dots. Never had she looked lovelier.

Punch. His inner world spun. Suddenly, the scorching heat didn't bother him. Conrad inhaled deep, drinking in all things Jane. Honeysuckle and roses. Magnolia and gardenia. Home.

In the dictionary of his life, a mental picture of this moment would forever hang alongside the words *peace* and *joy*.

Desperate to get closer to her, he carried his bag of supplies to the porch.

"I made snacks," she said with her customary sunny smile. "Hungry? Thirsty?"

He couldn't tear his gaze away. "Very much so," he muttered.

Pink circles bloomed over the rise of her cheeks as they stared at each other. For Conrad, nothing else existed. Until Beau exited the house, a man on a mission.

The vet stopped when he noticed the bag filled with goodies from Pan Out Hardware hanging from Conrad's arm. "Locks?"

"Among other things."

"Exactly what I was on my way to get." The other man redistributed the bag to his own grip. "I'm working on the windows in the primary bedroom." He glanced between Conrad and Jane, then rolled his eyes, grabbed a few items from the tray, and stepped inside, calling, "Come help when you escape the Ladling Vortex."

The exchange struck Conrad as genuine and friendly. His admiration for the guy reached new heights.

"Pay him no mind," Jane said with a chiding tone. "As if anyone can escape my clutches."

He snorted, charmed all over again, and looked over the tray. Glasses of iced tea, a plate of finger sandwiches cut exactly like those she'd gobbled up at Hotchkins's memorial, a bowl filled with what appeared to be sugar-glazed scones, a small jar of black jam and an even smaller jar of whipped cream. Plus napkins and plates. A spread worthy of a king.

"Cucumber and herbed cream cheese sandwiches, honey butter scones, blueberry lemon jam and vanilla whipped cream. I made everything myself." She placed the tray on a small table between the rockers, then sat gracefully and motioned to the other chair. "Well, I didn't churn the butter or anything like that. Anyway. If you hate something, I just want you to know that means your taste buds are dead. Every dish is amazing and definitely the best in the world probably."

She'd made all this herself? Dazed, he strode over and eased down. A slight tremor plagued his hand as he accepted a glass of tea. Very sweet tea, he realized after the first sip. Wow. Instant sugar high.

She put together a plate and passed it his way with a soft smile. "Thank you for rushing over to help me. I appreciate you greatly."

He...didn't know what to say. Had anyone ever taken such time and effort to appreciate him for something he'd done? Overcome by an emotion he couldn't name, he turned his attention to the food. Oh wow. Every bite proved better than the last, his taste buds exploding with a wealth of fresh flavors.

"This is amazing, Jane."

"Well, you're a pretty amazing man," she replied in a gentle tone.

The compliment shot straight to his head. They peered at each other again, each of them smiling, until the sound of metal clanging against metal pierced the air.

"Rolex, you little—" Beau's voice traveled from an open window upstairs.

Jane pressed a palm over her heart. "He's such a perfect, playful cat."

Perfect wasn't exactly the word Conrad would use to describe the murderous mini-beast. "I better go help."

"Of course. I'll show you the way." All grace and elegance, Jane flowed to her feet and led him inside.

Cool air enveloped him. He wanted to look around, but he also had zero desire to glance away from Jane. Her hips swayed as they made their way up the creaking stairs and entered a small, cluttered bedroom. What the... So. Many. Hats. Pink and purple everywhere. The curtains. The quilt covering the bed. He swallowed. He even spotted a pink and purple cushion under a mountain of clothes.

Rolex perched on the bed, staring at Beau, who knelt in front of the only window. The feline slowly craned his head in Conrad's direction and hissed.

Need the little criminal's approval if I'm going to date his mother. Ignoring him for now—what else could he do?— Conrad selected the proper tools from the array lined up on the floor and concentrated on the doorknob. The lock had rusted.

"Do you even know what you're doing?" Beau asked him as Jane settled beside her cat to scratch the little monster behind his ears.

"I do. In my spare time, I like to tinker with Stella."

The other man snorted. "Please don't tell me that's a lady robot."

Conrad snorted right back. "She's my kit car. Well, part kit car, part my own design. Right now I'm scouring the internet for an antique spoiler and...I've lost you both, haven't I?"

A pause. Then, "Cars aren't my thing," Beau admitted. "I prefer to work with wood. I've gotten good at birdhouses and squirrel feeders."

Conrad joked, "Not a manly and rugged hobby like mine, but not bad either."

They snickered at each other, as if they were buddies. Maybe they were. He knew he admired the man, and wasn't that the first step?

Lapsing into silence, they finished both upstairs bedrooms and moved on to the downstairs guest bedroom. A delightful room. Inviting, with a large brass bed covered by a mostly yellow patchwork quilt. Atop a hand painted dresser sat a basket of half-completed funny bunnies.

"Anyone work up an appetite yet?" Jane said. "I have all the ingredients for cheese straws, chicken salad sandwiches and blueberry cobbler." She didn't wait for a reply, but dashed off.

The second they were alone, Conrad said, "I already told her I want the security feed, so now I'll tell you. I expect it today." Rather than remind Jane of the incident, forcing her to relive her terror, he went straight to the source.

"One step ahead of you. I emailed you a link before we finished the last room."

Okay. "Appreciate it."

They were getting started on the front door locks in the living room when their adorable hostess announced the promised snacks were ready. In the kitchen, a veritable spread covered the peninsula. Besides the sandwiches, straws, and leftovers from the tray, she'd added asparagus wrapped in some kind of puffed-up bread, and the other food group: fried. Fried okra, fried pickles, and fried green beans.

Conrad couldn't not stuff his face. Every bite tasted better than the last. "I might have to double my jog time after this," he muttered.

"You're a jogger? That's cute." Beau seized a couple cheese straws. "I lift weights. Big ones. Huge."

"Enjoy joint replacement surgery in a few years." Conrad plucked the remaining straws off the platter.

He would swear Beau almost laughed. "When I go camping, I only take a knife. It's all I need." The vet's challenging tone proclaimed, *Beat that.*

"When *I* go camping, I take my bare hands."

They shared another snicker.

"All right. We'll settle the battle of the toughest with football," Conrad said. "Tell me your team."

"Georgia Bulldogs."

"Tech Yellow Jackets."

They both chuckled. Rivals.

Beau took a drink of sweet tea. "Enjoy losing this season."

What did Jane think of this? Conrad peered her way and chuckled all over again. She wasn't even listening. Instead, she stared faraway, lost in thought. When a radiant smile lit her lovely face, he couldn't help but draw nearer to her. Oh, the things he would give to peek inside her brain.

"Leave her to her daydream," Beau said with a quiet tone. "Let's finish up."

Walking away proved difficult, but he did it. As soon as he and Beau replaced every lock and bolt in the cottage, Conrad said his goodbyes and headed to his vehicle. He wanted to remain, but he needed to work. Who murdered Hotchkins, and who broke in her house. His fingers tightened around the steering wheel at even the thought of someone disrupting her peace of mind.

At home, he didn't bother getting comfortable. He just sat down and watched the security feed the vet had sent him. The intruder wore a dark hooded jacket and gloves, plus a black and white skeleton mask and ratty brown wig. About the size of Tiffany Hotchkins and Emma Miller. Too short to be Caroline Whittington. Or Anthony Miller or Dr. Garcia in disguise.

Whoever she was, she entered the house with a key and flew out within minutes. Didn't seem to be holding or carrying anything. A homicidal Rolex jetted after her, giving chase.

Okay. All right. Conrad absolutely saw the feline's appeal. The sweet little darling.

He fast-forwarded to Fiona's arrival but returned to normal speed upon Jane's. The two women spoke before Jane rushed inside the house. Wasn't long before she rushed back out, searching for her beloved baby. The anguish in her expression nearly unmanned Conrad.

Did the break-in have anything to do with the case? It must. And he must solve it. Fast.

The next morning, he returned to Aurelian Hills Medical Clinic, determined to gain answers. "I'm here to see Emma Miller and Caroline Whittington," he said. Patients in the lobby gaped at him as if he'd beamed down from a spaceship. Strangers stood out here, law enforcement more so.

The receptionist jumped to her feet and hurried to show him to an exam room.

"Someone will be with you soon," she muttered, shutting the door.

The room didn't appear different from any of the others he'd visited in the past. Same beige walls featuring framed licenses from the Georgia Composite Medical Board, a paper wrapper draped over the examination table, and some kind of water stain on a ceiling tile. Did this particular stain indicate money problems?

Caroline Whittington entered within minutes, her red hair scooped away from her face. Like before, she wore a pair of pale green scrubs. After washing her hands at a sink near the door, she approached him. "Emma has the day off," she said, cool as could be. "How may I help you, Agent?"

He decided to start with a bang. "Did you sleep with Dr. Hotchkins?"

Appearing horrified, she jerked back. "Me? No! Of course not. He was a married man. And why would I gift you with his disgusting little black book if I was featured in it?"

Something he, too, had wondered. One answer struck him as possible: Someone desperate enough to add a host of other suspects, even at the expense of her secret. "Did you hunt gold with him?"

"Me?" she repeated, thumping her chest. "Do you know how much free time I don't have, agent? Any free minutes I manage to steal, I use to research cures for cancer. I didn't save my father, but I promise you I'll not stop until I'm able to help another daughter on the verge of losing everything dear to her."

A tragic tale he planned to verify, but the depth of grief in her eyes told him she'd spoken true. Still. He didn't trust her. Or any of the others. "You were overheard whispering with Dr. Hotchkins at Summerhill Pediatric." A misleading statement. Dr. Holmgren had heard the word *muffin*, something that had nothing or everything to do with the case. How would Whittington respond?

Her level of incredulity heightened. Mumbling under her breath, she pinched the bridge of her nose. "I remember the instance you're referring to because it's the only time we ever whispered together. We were discussing Abigail Waynes-Kirkland. Earlier that morning, I ran into her at The Grind. She kept asking me questions about Dr. Hotchkins and gold. Had he found some. Did he ever mention a map. I told him what she said, and he told me not to worry about it, that he was taking care of Ms. Muffins himself."

Ms. Muffins. Not a plot to meet at a dog's headstone, but confirmation of a nickname. No doubt they'd find it among the un-decoded names in the planner.

"I immediately chided him for using such an awful nickname, of course," she continued with a huff. "Did the eavesdropper tell you *that* part?"

"She did not," he replied, resisting the urge to sigh. If the PA was telling the truth, his theory had just crashed and burned.

A text came in, saving him from asking any other rash questions. He made a big show of pulling his phone from his pocket, all *this is important GBH agent business*. "Thank you for your time," he told her, and aimed for the door. "I'll be in touch."

Once back in his car, he read the message.

Boss: Subpoena is in. I'm sending in a team.

Excellent. He could speak with Emma Miller and Dr. Garcia after techs combed their cellular devices. In the meantime, he could turn his attention to Abigail Waynes-Kirkland. The alleged Ms. Muffins.

CHAPTER TEN

Want to be irresistible? Look at her as if she's the only snack
in the world, and you're starving.
    –A Gravekeeper's Guide to Dating

*C*onrad stepped into Gilt, the art gallery that
employed Abigail Waynes-Kirkland. A bell jingled
above the door, welcoming him into an open space. In a
blink, he left the sizzling sunlight scented with car exhaust
and entered frigid air conditioning coated with expensive
perfume.

The old storefront had been transformed into a sterile
showplace. A dull gray infected everything from the ceiling
to the floor. Other than the artwork, the only bit of color
came from black barreled track lighting. A grand total of
zero customers walked about. He could understand why
'closing soon' signs filled the outer windows. Horrible paintings decorated the walls. The absolute worst. Over-the-top
experimental statement pieces.

The clack of high heels sounded, heralding the arrival of a
pretty brunette. She rounded a corner wearing a tight black

dress, carrying herself as if she balanced a book on her head. Abigail Waynes-Kirkland. An older, more sophisticated version of her mugshot, taken at the age of eighteen, after she vandalized the shops located in this very building, owned by her mother.

She was similar in size to the widow Hotchkins and Nurse Miller. What if *she* had broken into Jane's?

"Welcome," she said, spreading her arms to emphasize the entire gallery. "Are you here for something particular?"

"I am. I'm here to speak with you." He shifted the lapel of his suit jacket to reveal his badge. "I'm Special Agent Ryan. I'd like to clarify some details concerning your relationship with Dr. Marcus Hotchkins."

She nearly missed her next step. But she recovered quickly, pasting a bright if brittle smile on her face. "What's there to clarify? I didn't have a relationship with Mark. Marcus. He was my best friend's husband, and I spoke to him occasionally."

So she'd decided to kick things off with a lie. He removed his sunglasses, saying, "Good to hear. You have nothing to fear, then, as my team finishes their deep dive into every aspect of the doctor's life. Currently they're following a financial trail that leads straight to the doors of his many mistresses. Those who lie about a connection to him are being brought in for formal questioning. But like I said, you have no reason to fear."

Paling, she shifted from one foot to the other. "I might have, maybe, possibly—hypothetically—met him at a motel a few times. But only a few times, and I always felt horribly guilty afterward. But you can't tell Tiff! She'll never forgive me, and she needs me right now. She's never needed anyone more."

The same selfish, deceitful logic he'd heard from admitted killers. "Did you treasure hunt with the doctor?"

"No!" she assured him a little too swiftly.

No elaboration? "At the Grind, you questioned Caroline Whittington regarding the doctor's gold, did you not?"

Her eyes narrowed. "I said I didn't hunt with him, not that I'm ignorant of the gold. Tiff mentioned his obsession a few times. And my friend Emma Miller—she works with him. We had a little too much to drink one night, and she told me how she found a nugget in Mark's pocket. I just wondered if anyone else had seen it, that's all. I thought I could maybe, I don't know, find my own and save my mother's gallery."

Emma Miller again. Her fingers were in every pot.

"Hey," Waynes-Kirkland piped up. "Whoever killed Mark must have carried him to the cemetery to bury him. He never would have stepped foot on the property otherwise. He feared death. That's why he worked so hard to keep his patients alive. Now, do I look like I can lift a body? And risk breaking a nail to dig a hole? Never."

Fear of death? This was the first Conrad had heard of it. Was she spinning a tale for him...or had Hotchkins spun a tale for her? "Have you visited the Garden of Memories recently?"

"The cemetery?" Her face scrunched with disgust. "No. Gross." She backed away from him, her brittle smile reappearing. "Are we done here?"

For now. "Thank you for your time. I'll call you if I have any further questions."

"And I'll answer, promise." She waved him off.

Sighing, Conrad strode from the building. He drove back to Atlanta, determined to gather everything he needed to arm himself for tomorrow's confrontation. Another conversation with Mrs. Miller.

LATE THE NEXT MORNING, Conrad and Barrow hopped in an SUV to return to Aurelian Hills. A gloomy sky promised a storm at any moment. Not that the other agent cared. He sat behind the wheel, beaming all kinds of sunshine as he talked up his kids.

They had two tasks to complete today. Remove the crime scene tape at the Garden and speak with Emma Miller.

Sure, someone else could perform the first, but the thought of seeing Jane again... Yeah. Conrad needed to see her.

A text pinged his phone, and he checked the screen. Jane. He grinned. Had she sensed his thoughts?

He read the message, his grin fading.

> Jane: Ran into Dr. Garcia (not my fault!) We chatted. He says he's innocent. I also bumped into Abigail Waynes-Kirkland at Gold Fever! She thinks there's gold buried in my cemetery. She heard it from Tiffany, who read Dr. Hotchkins's notes about it. Thoughts??????

All this happened today? Conrad pinched the bridge of his nose. So. Waynes-Kirkland was more of a gold hunter than she'd copped to. Was she the one who'd broken into Jane's home or not?

He jabbed a fingertip at the screen of his phone, typing in all caps. *MY THOUGHTS ARE NOT FIT FOR TEXTING.* Then he deleted it. Jane might take those words as flirting rather than a stern rebuke.

Therefore, he typed a straight up rebuke. Deleted it. How

could he chide Jane for being, well...Jane? The quality he admired most about her?

Finally he settled on a single word: *Thanks.*

No encouragement, but no chastisement, either. As the seconds passed, however, he stewed in worry. He typed up a second text. *Are you being safe? Legit gold or not, the mere suspicion puts you in danger.*

> Jane: Super safe!

He saw bubbles. What would she say next? Another admission of case interference? Wait. The bubbles vanished. Then they reappeared. Nope. Gone again.

Frustration scraped at already raw nerves. "I need to make a call," he muttered to Barrow, interrupting the man's boast about a judo match. With the tap of his finger, Conrad dialed Miss Jane Ladling.

"I assure you," she began in lieu of a greeting.

"You're typing too slow," he said. He made no mention of his location: soon to arrive at the cemetery. "Just tell me what's going on."

"Um, so, quick detail, no big deal, because there's no way it's a crime since I did the right thing, given the circumstances and information at hand, so don't even think about arresting me, but I kind of punched Dr. Garcia in the face before we chatted."

What! Conrad squeezed his phone. What had the doctor done to deserve a strike from the (sometimes) gentle gravekeeper? "Start from the beginning. I want to know every detail concerning both encounters. Waynes-Kirkland and Garcia." What happened?

"Well. You see, I was walking down the sidewalk in town, minding my own business mostly when all of the sudden someone snatched my arm and pulled me into an alley. I reacted on instinct, as anyone would, and swung. Boom! Suddenly he's got a broken nose and blood is pouring. But like I said, there's no way this is a crime because it was self-defense on my part. Mostly. I mean, he didn't do anything bad. And Grandma Lily did tell me again and again to season my words and actions with grace. Grace doesn't punch all willy nilly. And really, he just wanted me to know that he's innocent, but he'd had a terrible fight with Dr. Hots the day of the murder—did you know Dr. Garcia hoped to buy the clinic and get rid of the serial banger? Anyway. You guys took all their electronics or something, so he's certain he's going to prison."

When she finished, she drew a deep breath, as if gearing up for another speech. The only way Conrad could react? Release a sigh from the depths of his being. What was he going to do with this woman?

"Do you have plans tonight?" he asked.

"A date?" Barrow whispered.

Conrad waved the question away as a crackling pause stretched between him and Jane.

"Are you about to ask me on a real date?" she rasped, excitement dripping from her tone. "Because I might say yes, even though I really, really should say no. And not just because of the case."

That excitement... Any lingering upset drained from him. "I'll take that as a no, you have no plans, so I'll be over at seven. I'll bring dinner, and you'll explain this mysterious reason to reject me." The supposed curse? "Dress comfortably. This isn't a date—" not officially—"but a training seminar." Because of the investigation, that's the way it had to be. "You'll be learning how to defend yourself on purpose."

"I accept your command/request, but don't bring food." Her excitement only magnified. "I'll cook."

The call ended before he could tell her about his plans to remove the crime scene tape.

"Not a date, huh?" Barrow grinned a little too widely. "Simply giving away free self-defense lessons?"

Conrad responded with a grumbling sound.

"That's how all long-lasting relationships start, by the way," his partner said, his wide shoulders shaking in laughter.

Ignoring the man, Conrad texted Beau: *Be on the lookout. If the Garden gets any visitors in the next few days, I want to know about it. There are more treasure hunters in AH than previously suspected.*

> B. Harden: I'll add alarms to Jane's windows and doors. If anyone breaches the house, I'll receive an alert.

Good man.

> Conrad: I'll be there at 7, and I'll be double checking your work.

> B. Harden: Hilarious. As if you'll even understand half the things I've done.

He chuckled. A short while later, he and Barrow reached the cemetery. No sign of Jane. Though he spotted Beau's truck parked near the cottage, Conrad never encountered him as he cleared the murder scene for visitors. He didn't remove the cameras at Muffin's headstone. Not yet, anyway. No one had taken the bait and come to collect the false murder weapon. But they could, now that GBH seemed to be backing off.

At the clinic, they discovered Emma had gone home sick. Thankfully, it wasn't a wasted trip. Garcia had returned, and Conrad used the opportunity to warn the doctor: Do not approach Jane again. The man sported a broken nose, which had caused two black eyes. Good. Perhaps he'd learned the error of his ways.

"Do we wait for Mrs. Miller to recover?" Barrow asked as they climbed into the SUV. "If she's truly sick."

"Only one way to find out. We have to risk it." But she wasn't at home, or she wasn't answering.

Time to make this official.

He phoned her and went straight to voice mail. He left a message, requesting a response from her or her attorney by morning.

Back at GBH offices, he assigned Hightower the chore of monitoring the Headliner for any new references to gold. Something he would have done himself if he hadn't had a date-non-date. Then Conrad drove home, showered and dressed in a T-shirt and jeans. A sense of anticipation grew as he returned to the Garden. By the time he arrived, he practically shook with it.

He parked in the clearing in front of the cottage. Beau's truck was gone, and the hearse was in its usual space. A notification for a text popped up on his phone.

> Hightower: 11 people were discussing the possibility of gold being found in the cemetery this afternoon. 6 haven't stopped.

Eleven. Eleven potential treasure hunters casing the Garden. And what of those who *weren't* posting? He went stiff as a board.

He replied: *Let me know if anyone decides to act.*

Beau's truck eased next to his sedan. Here for dinner, too? Hmm. Did Jane invite him as a buffer? Or had Beau come without an invitation?

They exited at the same time. The guy wore a T-shirt and shorts and held a duffel bag. No invitation, Conrad decided.

This was payback for the crack about checking the guy's work.

"You waited until seven on purpose," he said with a roll of his eyes. "Admit it."

Smug, Beau responded, "Isn't my presence admission enough?"

They made their way to the porch in companionable silence. Conrad knocked, giving two hard raps of his knuckles, and it wasn't long before hinges were squeaking, the most incredible scents drifting from the house. His mouth watered. Then he spotted Jane, and his mouth watered for a different reason. She wore a tank top and shorts beneath a ruffled apron, her mass of dark hair anchored in a ponytail.

Punch. How adorable was she?

Rolex sat at her feet. He hissed at Conrad, then Beau.

"Don't mind me," the vet said. "I'll be installing an alarm system from wall to wall, floor to ceiling." With a nod, he marched inside, disappearing beyond the door.

Jane wrinkled her nose, calling, "Not unless I get a bill first. Which you can give me at dinner. Which you are eating with us, so don't even consider saying no." She motioned Conrad inside. "You told him about Dr. Garcia, I take it?" Accusation tinged her tone.

"I did not." He entered the house. "I informed him of the gold hunters. As he is your security guard, I believed he needed to be in the know. I made a judgment call. The real question is, why didn't you tell him?"

She backed up, maintaining distance between them, raised her chin and squared her shoulders. A soldier ready for battle. "I won't take advantage of our friendship."

Too bad. "When it involves your safety, scales cease to matter." He shut and locked the door without looking away from her. "Why is there a scale between you and Beau in the first place?" Blood heating, he leaned into her. "Until I catch the killer, let Beau help you every way he can. Okay?"

Would she allow the nearness? Perhaps even approach him on her own?

Chewing on her bottom lip, she...did. She eased into his personal space to sniff him, and he nearly barked out a laugh. Then she straightened with a snap, as if she'd just come to her senses.

"I know why Beau decided he liked you," she said. "But what flipped the switch from animal-kingdom rules to bro code for *you*?"

A subject for a day. "Do you really want to discuss it?" His voice dipped. "Or would you rather hear my thoughts about you instead?" Her reason for rejecting him waited in their discussion queue amid a host of other topics. But he preferred to save that particular topic for a time when they were alone.

Their gazes remained locked. Her pupils expanded, and her lips parted. He loved how strongly he affected her.

"I don't need you to tell me," she said, raising her chin another notch. "I can guess your thoughts about me. Too curious. Too superstitious about curses. And fun." Her brow lifted as her irises sparkled with sudden amusement. "Am I right? I'm right, aren't I?"

Oh, to see that sparkle every day for the rest of his life.

He jolted. Permanence? For him? A lump grew in his throat. "Sorry, but I deem my impressions of you classified until the case closes." He untied her apron, because he needed something to do with his hands. "The food smells amazing. Let's eat."

She sputtered for a moment. "You're gonna end the conversation like that?"

Without a doubt.

Conrad winked at her, as if he hadn't lost all his cool, and sauntered farther inside. Jane darted ahead to lead the way to the dining room. Rolex perched in the table's centerpiece bowl, watching him. Beau was busy laying out his tools and equipment on the yellow counter that divided the two spaces.

"Sit, sit," she said, motioning to the dining room chairs.

Conrad obeyed, and she hastened to a china cabinet to fetch another plate. As soon as she'd added a third place setting across from him, Beau also reluctantly obeyed. Humming under her breath, she donned oven mitts and began bringing in dishes. One after the other. Her guests could only gape.

"I've never seen anything like this." An absolute feast of goodness. The kind a family of six or more would reserve for special occasions. There were multiple casseroles, mashed this and creamed that, with steamed and fried vegetables next to sauces of every consistency and color.

"Are you expecting other guests?" Beau asked, clearly as awed as Conrad.

"Nope. Just us. Why?" She took the seat between them and scooped a bit of everything onto their plates. "Oh, and make sure to save room for dessert. I baked your favorite pie."

He gave himself an inner shake. "I'm curious. What's my favorite pie?" And how had she learned what it was when *he* wasn't sure? He usually avoided carbs.

"I don't know." Again, her eyes twinkled at him. "We'll find out together."

There was no stopping his smile. *I am not falling for this woman. I've already fallen.*

The thought rocked him to his core. Maybe she experienced something similar. A flush spread over her cheeks. He felt himself lean toward her again, ready to press his lips into hers. She leaned toward him.

Beau coughed and adjusted the neckline of his shirt. "I get that you guys are having a moment, but I'm starved. Mind if I dive in?" He rubbed his hands together as Conrad and Jane came to their senses.

A little laugh left her. Did she have any idea what direction Conrad had hoped to go? How would she react if he told her?

Should he tell her? That curse...

"Please do dive in," she said, filling her own plate.

Noticing the bruises that discolored her hand, he tenderly cupped her fingertips to inspect the injury. No swelling, so no broken bones. Pride filled him. She'd made a proper fist and protected herself well.

"You blackened both his eyes." He gently grazed his thumb over her battered knuckles. "Good job."

"Are black eyes better or worse than a broken nose?" she asked, sounding worried.

"The broken nose caused the black eyes, making them equal."

Her worry melted away, her own sense of pride blossoming. "My first time throwing a punch, and I hit the bull's eye."

Oh, yeah. He had definitely fallen for this woman.

"If someone ever grabs you again, go for their throat and run away screaming," Beau said, after swallowing a bite of a casserole. "You will run away screaming, won't you, Jane?"

"As fast as your feet can carry you," Conrad commanded. "Screaming loudly." With Jane, it was best to cover every base.

Trepidation flashed inside her baby blues. "You guys expect more trouble, don't you?"

He would take no chances with her. "I have an agent monitoring the Headliner. As of this afternoon, eleven people have mentioned the possibility of finding gold in your cemetery."

Yes, the rumors about gold were old, and treasure hunters had searched here in the past, but. You only needed one to wreak havoc on Jane's life. "Those eleven will tell others. Those people will spread the word further. At some point, someone will sneak onto your property to find out the truth."

Radiating ferocity, Beau said, "Whatever day it is, whatever time, I want you to call me at even the hint of a trespasser."

Jane nodded, but Conrad wasn't sure he believed she'd make the call. She needed those self-defense lessons more than ever.

He devoured his meal, both hurrying, eager to begin her training, and savoring, floored by the perfection of flavors. Never had he enjoyed food more. Though full, Conrad sampled each dessert and decided his favorite pie was all of them.

"I'll clean up," he said.

"I'll help," Beau announced.

"As if!" Jane wagged a finger at them. "Grandma Lily will roll over in her grave if I shirk my duties."

"Or she'll applaud our willingness to perform *our* duties." No way he sat back and watched his hostess clean after she'd done the cooking. Unwilling to entertain further arguments, he stood, gathered what dishes he could, and strode to the sink.

Beau followed. They washed and dried while a sputtering Jane delivered the rest of the dirties.

They were a team, and it was kind of wonderful.

When they finished, Conrad focused fully on Jane. "Beau has a lot to do—" hint, hint—"and I have a lot to teach you. We should get started."

The vet snickered before returning his attention to his equipment.

"Let's go out back," Conrad suggested, beyond ready to have her to himself.

She led him to the porch, where a bulb illuminated soft grass and billowing trees. Lightning bugs flashed here and there, creating an almost magical backdrop. The incredible scent of magnolia filled his nose and fogged his head. For the rest of his life, he would associate magnolia with Jane Ladling.

As he focused on her, his eagerness nearly spilled over. "Let's begin."

CHAPTER ELEVEN

Always sometimes display a secret playful side. This will
keep certain gravekeepers on their toes.
—A Gravekeeper's Guide to Dating

*T*his might have been a huge mistake.

Conrad moved behind Jane to adjust her posi-
tion for the coming "attack." Her flowery scent remained in
his nose, a temptation like no other. The fact that he was
about to put his hands on her soft skin and perfect curves,
after he'd just admitted to catching feelings in the middle of a
homicide investigation, pushed his control to the brink of
collapse.

"Like that," he muttered, returning to his post in front
of her.

"Got it." With her legs braced apart, her fists up and her
expression etched with determination, she reminded him of
a cupcake with the word KILLER scripted across the icing.

Might have been a mistake? Might! He wasn't sure he
would survive this encounter.

"Ready?" He jumped from side to side while popping

bones in his neck, pretending to wait for her response. Only, he didn't wait. He lunged.

She yelped as he drove her to the springy grass. And yes, he ensured she landed gently. Hovering over her, he nearly kissed her before he chided, "You've got to be ready even when you're not ready." He flowed to his feet and pulled her to hers. "We'll try this again." Until she executed a perfect block by rote.

"I'll be read—eek!"

Conrad took her down a second time. As she gaped up at him, he arched a brow. "You were saying?"

She opened and closed her mouth. He straightened and helped her to her feet again. Smoothing her garments in place, she said, "Yes. Well. Perhaps I'm luring you into a false sense of calm."

He prowled around her, a predator who'd cornered prey. "Consider me extremely calm." Whoosh. Down she went.

"Oh!" she fumed, lightly beating her fists into his shoulders. "You are showing off, and I am loving it!"

Snorting, he drew her to a stand. Her flirty words hadn't matched her irritated tone, and the contrast proved as delightfully contradictory as the rest of her. "All right. This time, we go in slow motion. I attack, you defend with a little something I call the Testicle Relocator." He showed her the move. "You do what I did, okay? Tell me your thought process every step of the way."

"Okay, yes." She nodded, eager. "This will be fun."

Or torturous. "Here goes."

As Conrad exaggerated his movements, she said, "I'm thinking oh dear, trouble found me. Look at those biceps. Wow! No, no. Concentrate. I'm supposed to stop him. With a one-two strike? Yes!" She acted out the motion.

"Very good," he said, fighting a grin. A common occurrence in her presence.

"Very good," she replied, mocking him. But even that was done politely.

He barked a laugh. "Now, we do it again and again and again, picking up the pace as warranted." And that was exactly what they did.

He took his job seriously and worked with her, relentless in his precision. She surprised him over and over by absorbing instruction or correction and adapting, improving by leaps and bounds. All the while, they shared an easy back and forth, every part of him excited to be alive, helping this woman in some way, enhancing her life as she'd enhanced his.

"You're a natural," he praised.

She preened, making his freaking heart skip a beat.

He rasped, "That's enough for one night."

Disappointment flickered in her eyes, but she didn't protest. In silence, they ambled into the house, where Beau was busy gathering his tools.

"Thank you so much for your time and energy," she told her friend, ever gracious. "Oh, and your dohickey majigs."

Dohickey majigs? As in, the things he'd added to the locks? "Yes, thank you," Conrad reiterated, meaning those words from his deepest depths. Rivals or not, friends or not, the vet had made Jane's safety and well-being a priority. He must give respect where respect was due.

"Anytime. See you two later." Beau nodded at them on his way out the door.

For the first time, Conrad detected total acceptance from the guy. Far more than a concession. There was no question the other male had relinquished any lingering romantic aspirations toward Jane and only sibling love remained.

Relief poured through Conrad as Jane issued a sunny wave and called, "Okay, bye."

He kept his attention on the gravekeeper… who quickly

sensed his intensity and shivered. Her gaze slowly slid to his, and her lips parted. A brand-new flush spread over her cheeks.

He entered her personal space, unable to stay away, and traced his knuckles over her jawline. Goose bumps traveled over her skin, thrilling him. He winked and smiled. "Try not to miss me too much." He severed contact and turned before he did something even more foolish.

Voice sweetness and light, she called, "Don't die on your way home."

Another laugh escaped him. Anyone else would have layered those words with sarcasm. Not his Jane. She meant them in earnest. "Goodnight, Jane."

"Goodnight, Conrad."

He climbed into his car. His headlights flashed over her as he maneuvered from the driveway. She remained on the porch, a vision sweeter than the tea she liked to serve.

Relationship complications plagued him the entire drive home. Better to deal with his feelings from the start. Yes, he had fallen for her. No, they'd never even gone on a date. No, he didn't know how she felt about him. Not officially. But he recognized special when it showed up in his life. Why not fight for it? Despite the distance between them. Despite the curse, whatever it was. Finally he could have everything he hadn't known he wanted. Because yes, he would succeed with her.

Something he'd learned: *Never enter a battle thinking you're destined to lose. Always go in confidant you won't stop until you win.*

He just needed to solve this case. A crime had been committed and a price must be paid. Then he could concentrate on his personal life.

After parking in his condo's garage, he checked his messages. Ah. A voice mail from Mrs. Miller's attorney.

"This is Devin Hagger. I'm representing Emma Miller. You want to talk to her, you have to talk to me first. We will *not* be meeting you bright and early in the morning. But I will accept your apology for overstepping when you call. We can discuss scheduling a formal conference mid-afternoon."

The guy came across as gruff, but it was nothing Conrad hadn't dealt with in the past. He knew the hiring of a lawyer meant little in terms of guilt or innocence. When heat turned on and pressure built, human nature sought a strong defense. He just wished people told the truth, whatever the consequences, because it was the right thing to do.

Conrad exited the car and headed inside his home. The quiet space with no character. Not something he'd ever resented... until now. After stripping to his underwear, he got comfortable in bed and opened his laptop to log into the Headliner. It wasn't long before he lost himself in a tsunami of gold-themed messages.

A little after 4:00 a.m., a notification popped up on his phone. The Garden Girl had just posted photos of—no she did not. But oh, she did. Filling his screen were images of an open casket. With a body inside it. A skeleton with hair, to be exact, dressed in a long black jacket, matching slacks, and a whiteish shirt with a wide, flat lapel. A silk bow circled the corpse's neck.

She'd actually dug this thing up. Next to the photos, she'd typed: *See? No gold at Garden of Memories. RIP Silas Ladling.*

Conrad counted to ten. Didn't help. Comments flooded in. As his blood pressure spiked, he collected screenshots of his top three favorites.

> John Langston: Believe Cemetery Girl's staged pictures? Try again.

> Mayor Donahue: You obviously removed the gold before taking those photos.

TripleR: Hahaha good one. Guess what? I'm a pro at Photoshop too.

TripleR then reposted a photo, except his version contained the coffin with gold nuggets spilling from its sides.

Conrad texted the screenshots to Jane before dialing her number. The second she picked up, he grated, "You dug up a body? With help from a certain someone, I'm sure." Enablers sucked!

A soft intake of her breath, barely detectable. "Why isn't your first guess looters," she asked, "since everyone in town has heard rumors about the gold?" Her low volume couldn't mask her curiosity. "I might have taken photos of their crime. In fact, I might be calling a certain special agent right now to report said crime. But however it happened, I think we can both agree it was my billion-year-old relative, my decision."

A rough sound escaped him. He'd lose his mind before they ever even went on their first date, and that was a fact. "We wanted to douse the flames of interest in the cemetery, not fan them."

"The coffin had no gold. Consider the flames doused. You're welcome, by the way." The irresistible mischief maker was patting herself on the back, wasn't she? "You can repay me by opening up my cemetery and removing the police tape."

He cringed. He'd forgotten to let her know he'd removed it. "First, I planned to call you in the morning and tell you the cemetery is cleared for visitors." He would have remembered by then. "Second, check out your text messages. I sent you multiple screenshots. Comments from your post."

Silence stretched between them as she complied. Then a new hitch of breath crackled over the line. "So that didn't go exactly as planned," she hedged. To his consternation, she still sounded hopeful. "How would *you* prove there's no gold here?"

He hid a groan within a sigh. She might have phrased those last words as a question, but he didn't miss the iron determination inside them. If that determination merged with her hope...look out world.

"I know this tone, Jane." He'd heard it every time she prepared to whisk him to the brink. "It means you're already plotting something else." He'd do whatever proved necessary to out-plot her. Even drive to the cottage and exhaust her with more self-defense lessons. Train until she dropped. "Stop it. Stop it right this second."

"I think I need to launch a sting operation," she stated, utterly unfazed. Truly, she sounded giddy.

He tried a different route. A simple, unmistakable negation, leaving no room for argument. "No." Wait. He was dealing with Jane Ladling here. Better to leave nothing for interpretation. "No sting operation, Jane."

She rolled into her next statement as if he'd never spoken. "I'll host a tour, like I've done countless times in the past. Business as usual. Except I'll charge double. Triple!" The giddiness intensified as she warmed up to her topic. "Prices so exorbitant they weed out the merely curious. Only people invested in the case or the gold will pay. And you can't forbid this, because the cemetery is still cleared for business, yes? Mourners gotta mourn, Conrad."

Hello, brink, my old pal. Though he hated to admit it, he grated, "Yes. You are still cleared to open your business." He must talk some sense into her. "What do you hope to learn from this?"

"Who's interested in the gold or the murder, as previously stated. Who's interested in the gold, period. If someone attempts to snag the murder weapon. Finally ending the mystery about the gold for everyone in town, making myself and my cat safer. Gaining a chance to look my home intruder in the eye. Revenge. Finding out if there's someone paranoid enough to double check that no evidence was left behind. Shall I go on?"

He huffed with irritation and grumbled, "How do you make sense?" Whatever. She did. "I can't believe I'm doing this." But. "Come to my office first thing in the morning. Eight sharp. If I can't stop your tour, I'll help you as much as I can." In fact, he would request a meeting with Ms. Randall at 7:00 a.m. to define his limitations.

"Thank you, Conrad. Thank you, thank you, thank you." Jane's renewed excitement spilled over the line.

He smiled. He would never not enjoy causing such a reaction from her. "Goodnight, Jane." He tried to make himself disconnect the call but failed. He wasn't ready.

Thankfully, she didn't hang up, either. "Something else you wanna say, Conrad?" A mix of hesitation and anticipation radiated through the phone.

This woman... she was the calm in his chaos. "I'm really glad I met you, sweetheart."

At first, she said nothing, and he wondered if he'd admitted too much too fast. Then she softly stated, "I'm glad I met you too."

His chest tightened. No, he wasn't in this alone. They hung up at last, and Conrad eased against the mound of pillows. Jane...in his office again... wearing a hat... He closed his eyes to savor the image.

The next thing he knew, the alarm on his phone erupted. Conrad bolted upright, confused and dazed. He'd slept two hours uninterrupted? Because he'd felt so close to Jane... whom he would see in only a matter of hours.

He shot a text to Ms. Randall, and sprang from the bed, energized. Today would be a great day.

CHAPTER TWELVE

You should forget to shave some mornings. But *only* if you want your five o'clock shadow to make you the hottest man alive.

–A Gravekeeper's Guide to Dating

*C*onrad strode from Ms. Randall's office and into his own, now armed and ready for his confrontation with Jane. Mostly ready. She had a way of throwing him for a loop during each and every interaction.

He removed his jacket, freed the top button of his shirt, ditched the cufflinks, and rolled up his sleeves. Then he sat behind the desk, his beloved tattoos on display. His gravekeeper seemed to have a special fascination with them.

Eight minutes and sixteen seconds until her arrival. If she arrived early, as usual. An attribute he greatly appreciated.

To check another item off his to do list, he phoned Devin Hagger and scheduled the meeting with Mrs. Miller for later that afternoon. And no, he did not apologize for doing his job.

Four minutes and forty-seven seconds.

Conrad fished his phone from his pocket and set the device on his desk. A message dominated the screen.

> Wyatt: How are things going with hat girl?
> Better than how things are going with Esme, I
> hope. She's my ex-ex-girlfriend BTW.

Hat girl?

What would it take to free Wyatt from his cycle of breakups? For that matter, what would it take to free Conrad from his?

He winced. He had a similar pattern. Only difference was, he never committed. He dated and ditched, sticking to what he knew. Being emotionally unavailable. Afraid of giving pieces of himself to someone he would lose later. Then Hurricane Jane had blown into his life, tearing the blinders from his eyes and ripping off prison doors in his mind, forcing him to face the truth. A relationship wasn't something to fear but embrace. A relationship meant... more. With Jane, he wanted, *needed*, what he'd never allowed himself to have. Connection.

Three minutes and two seconds. Where was she?

He shifted. Plowed his hands through his hair. Rubbed his jaw. Well. He'd forgotten to shave this morning. Unable to sit still, he flowed to his feet and opened the door. No sign of her in the hallway. Sighing, he moved to the edge of his desk, sat, and crossed his arms. Wait. Did he seriously want to look as though he'd purposely power-posed this?

Too late to reposition. Jane sailed into the office, head high, bringing the storm and the calm with her.

Punch. How did she grow more beautiful with every sighting? Today she wore a dress covered in colorful flowers. Perfect advertising. The woman smelled like a walking garden, the air in his office suddenly sweetened with an incredible array of magnolias, gardenias, and honeysuckle.

Mental note: *Buy a bulk order of floral scented candles.*

Voice thick, he said, "You're late."

She stopped short and rapid-blinked. "How?" Stealing a quick glance at the clock behind him, she said, "I'm two minutes early."

"Yes, but ten minutes early is the new on time, which makes you exactly eight minutes tardy," he deadpanned. For his sanity, he reclaimed his chair, putting the desk between them. "We should get started."

With all of her prim properness at the fore, she eased into a chair of her own. "We should indeed."

Adorable brat. "You look beautiful, by the way."

Pleasure wafted from her. Uncertainty followed. "Thank you." Flushing, she shifted, cleared her throat, and busied herself by flipping through the pages of a journal with the words Truth Be Told scrawled across the cover.

Not used to compliments? That was a shame and something in need of rectification. "All right," he said in a show of mercy. "Let's get to business. You know we have the camera on Muffin's marker. It's monitored twenty-four seven. There's no need for a tour."

"Actually, there is. Your camera has caught a big, fat nothing, I bet."

She wasn't wrong. But admit it aloud? No.

"What happened with the crowbar?" she asked.

All he could tell her? "It is indeed a murder weapon." It might not have caused Dr. Hotchkins to expel his last breath, but it caused the fall that had. Ergo murder weapon.

A bright, sunny smile bloomed. "It is? I did it, then? I found the most crucial piece of evidence in the entire case?"

Such earnest delight. His heart seemed to double in size. "The metal is splattered with Dr. Hotchkins's blood and covered with his fingerprints."

"Any other fingerprints?"

"None." He picked up a pen and tapped the edge against his desk. Time for their negotiation to officially kick off. "I think I've made it clear I don't want you to do the tour, Jane."

The little darling batted her lashes at him. "You have, yes, but it always sounds like a *you* problem."

Yet again, she wasn't wrong. Give him a moment, though, and he'd make it an *us* problem. "But," he said, forging ahead, "I can't stop you from doing it. If you insist on putting yourself in the line of danger, I will insist on doing something as well."

She practically melted in her seat.

Then he said, "I'll use you to draw the killer out," and her shoulders popped out. No doubt about it, the darling sleuth sensed his intent to take over and ruin her fun. "I think anything out of the ordinary will draw undue suspicion." He pushed the pamphlet she'd given him the day of the murder across the desk. "Scheduling a tour similar to this fits your profile."

"This? Are you kidding?" She gripped the trifold paper and waved it in the air. "A plain ole tour with no theme? Where's the drama?" she cried. "Everyone loves drama. Shouldn't we give the people what they want?"

"We don't care what other people want. We care about a killer. When should we ever cater to a killer?"

"Never," she grumbled, accepting another person's point of view, weighing the information against her own opinion, and choosing what was best for all. No wonder he adored her.

"Good girl. Now, you can make it seem like you're capitalizing on the unsolved murder or claim you can prove there's no hidden gold. Considering what you posted to the Headliner last night, the latter is more believable. You've gotten over fifty comments, each one accusing you of being a liar."

"My bad," she replied, wincing. "I'll go with the gold theme."

He gripped his chair to stop himself from reaching for her. "I will attend, of course, and I will—"

"No! Are you kidding?" She gaped at him. "The killer won't come if a GBH agent is there."

A killer would if a killer's curiosity about the case pulled his or her strings. "Nevertheless. I'll be buying a ticket. As a paying customer, I'll have every right to stand by your side, keeping you safe."

Different emotions flashed over her features. Awe. Tenderness. Aggravation. "Beau will be there. No one will try anything with him around. He's playing the part of groundskeeper."

"Then I'll be playing the part of Conrad, the groundskeeper's boss. And you're right. Many will recognize me. I want them to."

The aggravation upgraded to relish. "I can't wait to see you in the costume I plan to prepare for you."

Her form of vengeance delighted him as much as everything else about her. Make it easy on her, however? No. "The groundskeeper's boss doesn't require a costume."

"He's getting one anyway," she said, the relish downgrading to disappointment. "I'm putting a rush on this tour. Scheduling it for this weekend. You probably have plans—"

"I'll be there," he interjected. *Go ahead. Try to stop me. See what happens.*

A slight shiver cascaded over her. "Fine. Come as a paying guest. You'll not be getting a discount, so don't ask. Actually, your ticket has an out-of-town processing fee. Add a hundred dollars to it."

The *take that* tone of her voice sparked all kinds of warmth inside him. "Tell me who you expect to show up," he said.

He knew the second talk of the case lured her from her pique. Eager, she told him, "Emma Miller is my number one despite the supposed alibi you mentioned. Before the murder, she found out Dr. Hots was sleeping with other women. Dr. Garcia caught her crying."

Clever, clever Jane.

"Of course, he tops my list as well. So does Caroline Whittington and everyone else at the clinic. And also their significant others."

He appreciated a woman who covered every base. After a little checking, he'd learned Whittington's father had indeed died of cancer. But like Jane, Conrad still wasn't ruling out the physician assistant. Someone had to fund Whittington's research. What would be better than gold?

"Yes, but who's second on your list?" he teased.

She took him seriously, saying, "Abigail Waynes-Kirkland."

"Why her?" Did Jane know something he didn't?

"Three reasons. At the wake, she seemed bitter about his affairs. She cased the *Gold Fever!* exhibit, and she was close enough to the doctor to refer to him as Mark."

"Which is suspicious to you why?" he asked, digging deeper.

"She's the only one who uses such familiarity. It could mean they had an affair." Her eyes glazed, as if she'd gotten lost in her thoughts. Then she shook her head. A conversational reboot? "Have you heard of the Order of Seven?"

Reboot indeed. Thankfully, they'd circled back to the gold. "It may have come up in a meeting," he hedged.

"Well, allow me to captivate your imagination with what I know about it."

Finally!

"I did some digging," she said. "The Order of Seven was a secret society formed during the gold rush. An urban legend usually shared among teenagers. At the exhibit, Abigail studied one paper exclusively. A page referencing the Order. Here, I'll text you the photos I took of her and the page when I visited the museum against your wishes. It has the same base symbol that was spray painted all over town."

She lacked any semblance of shame as she fiddled with her phone. He huffed a breath when his cell phone vibrated, swiped up the device, and scanned the images she'd texted him. And she'd gotten excellent shots too?

Life wasn't fair.

Best not to encourage her. "Why am I just now seeing these photos?" he groused.

"I didn't know if the lead would pan out," she replied, far from intimidated. "Brilliant pun intended."

He preferred her previous method. Contact him the moment she suspected someone of something. "I want a copy of any documents you have."

"Sure. Because you requested so sweetly," she told him with a dry tone. "Abigail knew about the new gold supposedly stashed in my cemetery. Oh, and the same Order of Seven symbol is carved into the caskets of Rhonda Burgundy and Silas Ladling." Jane inched to the edge of her seat. "Silas Ladling's son was rumored to be a member of the Order. But he took a devastating financial hit when our mines petered out just as gold was discovered in California. In a matter of weeks, Aurelian Hills lost half its population. Businesses were suddenly without paying customers."

"And you think, what? That the Order is active again, the members searching for hidden gold?" One of the theories being entertained at GBH.

"Not necessarily. But Dr. Hotchkins did dabble in treasure hunting. You said so yourself. What if he had a partner who found something—outside my land, of course—who didn't want to share?" Pensive, she said, "To be honest, my gut is telling me a scorned lover did the deed."

"Almost eighty percent of killers are male," he said to discourage her from launching a new investigation. "That favors the gold angle." But only when considering the average number of male versus female hunters and only by a small percentage.

"Wow." She shook her head, as if disappointed in him. But oh how her eyes sparkled. "A woman is as capable and likely of committing a murder as a man, Conrad. We're just better at hiding it," she bragged.

He locked his hands behind his neck and leaned back in his chair. Not tease this woman? Impossible. "That's a brave thing for a former suspect to say to an officer of the law during an ongoing investigation."

Her breath caught. "When did I become a *former* suspect?"

For him? "When you looked at me with those big blue eyes."

She batted those big blue eyes at him now. "Am I a former suspect who qualifies for a tour of the crime lab?"

Ha! So persistent. "Your thought process fascinates me, but no. No tour. However, when this is over, I'll exchange a visit of the building for a visit of your mind. I'm taking a vacation and sitting down with you. I will ask questions, and you will answer. For days. We'll do other things too, but one way or another, I will learn all your secrets."

Her mouth floundered open and closed. Jane Ladling, speechless?

"Go home, Jane," he said, laughter bubbling in his tone. "Plan your event. I'll see you soon."

Delight flashed in her eyes. When she oh, so obviously forced a cough to mask it, he bit his tongue and (much more thoroughly) hid his own delight.

"Right," she said. "See you soon." Feigning nonchalance,

she offered him a casual wink. "Don't forget to buy your ticket and pay your out-of-town fee, agent. You won't be allowed in the cemetery otherwise."

A portion of a smile might have slipped free. He knew beyond any doubt she wanted him there, but oh, did he enjoy the games they played. "Jane, I doubt anything can keep me away from you."

CHAPTER THIRTEEN

Be careful who you trust with your hidden vulnerabilities.
Some people are wolves in sheep's clothing.
–A Gravekeeper's Guide to Dating

Conrad met Devin Hagger's hard stare. They occupied a small interview room at GBH headquarters, a camera recording their interaction. Emma Miller sat beside the attorney on one side of a table, with Barrow on the other next to Conrad. Two against two.

"Why are we here?" The sharpness of Hagger's question was meant to intimidate. But Conrad had faced irate, irrational foster fathers as a child; for the past decade, he'd gone toe to toe with gang leaders as well as lawyers who charged hundreds of thousands more than Aurelian Hills supposed best. He'd learned theatrics always attempted to cover insecurity.

Frankly, it surprised Conrad that Emma Miller had placed her future in the hands of her soon-to-be ex-husband's business partner. "A man's life was cut short. He deserves justice. We have questions, and she has answers that can help us get it for him."

Hagger thumped the table and shook his head. "There's justice, and there's entrapment. Your curiosity has no bearing on the situation. My client has more than proven her innocence."

This, Conrad was now prepared to refute. Not only with the motel clerk's testimony. The report on the little black book had come in a half an hour ago. Every nickname in the planner but one had been assigned to the proper recipient. Like any treasure hunter, Marcus Hotchkins had kept a key. Techs found it in a secret pocket of the planner's lining. The only member of the "buffet" the doctor had left off was the suspected gold hunter he'd referred to exclusively as Honeybun.

Yes, Hotchkins had met the hunter the night of his murder. Yes, she was a regular.

"Dr. Hotchkins named you Mashed Potatoes." Conrad directed his words to Mrs. Miller, who flinched. He could only guess at the reasons for assigning such an awful nickname to a woman the doctor had routinely bedded. "Maybe you knew, maybe you didn't."

Turned out, Abigail Waynes-Kirkland wasn't Ms. Muffins but Fried Okra.

The three chili peppers slash possible fleur-de-lys remained a thorn in Conrad's brain. Did it rate the spiciness of his sexual encounters, point to the treasure hunt, or represent a specific person? But which one? Honeybun or someone else? What about a *rival* gold hunter?

"I didn't hear a question," Hagger snapped, smoothing a hand over his balding head.

Conrad offered no reaction, keeping his attention on Miller. "Did you conspire with Dr. Garcia to murder Dr. Hotchkins, allowing Dr. Garcia to end a disastrous business

GENA SHOWALTER & JILL MONROE

relationship while you punished the man who helped ruin your marriage?"

The nurse bristled, a lock of hair falling from a severe bun. Gone were the colorful scrubs and perky ponytail. "I did no such thing. Yes, I slept with Marcus. Often. I admit it. It happened at the motel mostly, but sometimes at the clinic, after everyone else went home. But the night of the murder, I never left my house. Feel free to question my dog, Cheddar. He stayed with me."

"Let's say we believe you," Barrow said. "Let's say you and Dr. Garcia didn't leave the video chat running while you snuck out and met at the cemetery. Let's say he didn't kill Dr. Hotchkins while you cleaned up the mess. Who should we suspect?"

"Let's say you gather your own evidence and stop expecting my client to do your job for you," Hagger inter-jected with a scowl, squeezing the nurse's arm.

Miller pressed her lips together, remaining silent.

"Outline your day for us," Conrad said.

She glanced at Hagger, who released her and nodded. "My alarm is always set for six," she stated. "I fed Cheddar, cleaned up and dressed, then walked into the clinic around seven-thirty, for an eight o'clock open. Marcus and Caroline were already there."

A fact Conrad had known. "What were the doctor and PA doing?"

Her eyes brightened, as if a lightbulb had just gone off inside her mind. "You suspect Caroline? Yes, they totally could have slept together." Like a shark who'd scented blood; that's what she reminded him of. "He accidentally called her hon once. Caroline acted super mad but seemed pleased at the same time. I was so shocked to see the ice queen crack."

Hmm. Hon. Short for honeybun? Or simply a generic endearment Hotchkins used for random women? "To your knowledge, did he ever call anyone else hon? Or even honey?"

"No, but that doesn't mean anything." She wagged her jaw. "Now that I know he was a sex addict, I'm pretty confident *hon* was an endearment he used to make her think she was special to him. That she meant something." A note of bitterness seeped into her tone. "He called me *doll*. At least to my face," she added, grumbling.

Conrad's thoughts whirled. If Hotchkins and Whittington had an affair on top of hunting gold together, why keep her name off his key? He'd listed Emma, a fellow co-worker. And Whittington didn't have a significant other to hurt or infuriate. Why protect her privacy?

For the next half hour, Conrad and Barrow launched questions at Mrs. Miller, noting any inconsistencies with other statements. Finally, Hagger reached the limits of his patience.

The attorney exploded to his feet, saying, "That's enough. Either charge her with something, or we're done here."

"We're done here," Conrad offered easily.

Hagger flashed his teeth and helped Miller to her feet before marching to the door. Seconds later, the two were gone.

Conrad looked to Barrow. "Gotta admit, that went better than I expected." Everything inside him cried, *Finally on the right path.* "Let's look for anything honey related we might have missed in the planner."

"Will do," Barrow said with a nod.

Success was only a matter of time now. Well, that, and surveying Jane's event.

In the days before the Garden's scheduled midnight tour, Conrad questioned Whittington again. She claimed the doctor never referred to her as hon, honey or honeybun. Had Miller lied to him? The nurse had a habit of doing so. But how to prove it?

Conrad remained in contact with Beau via text. They mapped out a plan to keep Jane safe and secure despite her best efforts to rush headlong into danger. That was his excuse for showing up bright and early at the cottage the day of the event, anyway. Everything he needed for both labor and the party waited inside his car. The blond had beat him there and waited on the porch, sipping a glass of iced tea.

"Only an hour earlier than we planned?" Beau tsked and wagged his head, as if embarrassed for him. "Jane deserves better."

Conrad rolled his eyes. But he said, "I can't even argue with you."

They got busy hanging LED lanterns throughout the cemetery, creating predetermined paths for guests to walk. Anyone who deviated was going to be recorded with night vision cameras and watched by Barrow, who would be observing the festivities from a viewing station near the old business center.

When they finished that task, Conrad and Beau worked up a sweat constructing a small dais at the edge of the parking lot. The platform should provide a full view of the crowd—and offer a view of Jane's bodyguards. Another bonus: separating the lovely hostess from the masses.

With two hours to spare before kick off, they ambled to the cottage. As they entered, Jane blazed up the stairs, clad in a robe with curlers in her hair and a green mask on her face, the most adorable sight on Earth. Rolex trailed her as she called, "Whipped up some snacks for you. Feel free to use the guest room. Beau, I left the groundskeeper's costume on the bed. Okay, bye!" A door shut. A lock clicked.

Conrad stood there a moment, trying to collect his wits.

Beau snickered at him. "And I thought *I* once had it bad for her."

"You did. You just didn't have it bad *enough*."

The vet gave him a friendly shove. "Do you even hear yourself sometimes? Not bad enough," he mocked.

"Truth is truth." The scent of heaven drew them into the kitchen, where an array of dishes awaited them. Potato skins, loaded deviled eggs, hash brown sausage balls, ham and cheese sliders, crab cakes, and for dessert, Georgia peach cobbler. "Wow."

"How does so much food come out of such a small kitchen?"

After they gorged, they took turns showering. Conrad went first, dressing in all things GBH. A shirt with GBH embossed over the chest. Shiny badge hanging from a chain around his neck. And, despite the heat, he wore a wind jacket with the GBH emblem on the back, concealing his gun.

He returned to the kitchen to eat more cobbler, this time with two scoops of ice cream, and wait for his friend. Yeah, the description fit.

Beau, the poor sap, stalked in half an hour later wearing cuffed ultrashort shorts from the 70s and a too-tight ribbed T-shirt. His glare deepened as Conrad looked him over, a spoon halfway to his mouth.

A laugh burst from him. "I like your new look."

"Don't say anything el—"

"Behold," he announced, spreading his arms. "The gigolo groundskeeper."

The vet rubbed his face and grumbled, "Why am I doing this? Why?"

"Because you're a good friend."

"So why aren't *you* doing it?" the other man demanded.

"Because I'm a smarter boyfriend." Not that he and Jane—never mind.

"At the moment, I can't refute that." Beau gave himself a once over. "Obviously."

A stream of footsteps sounded. Fiona came flying down the stairs and into the room, calling, "Boys! Boys! Jane is ready for her grand entrance. Take your places." She clapped her hands before shoving a small piece of paper in Conrad's hand. "This is my number. Update me throughout the night, and I'll make my famous blueberry pancakes for you. Trust me, you'll never win my sweet Jay Bird without them. Now then." She clapped again, then shooed them both toward the bottom of the steps. "All right. We're ready for you, hon."

Ah. Okay. The dramatic movie entrance. Was there anything more Jane?

He shoved Fiona's number in his pocket, planning to contact her once an hour on the dot. Eager to see his grave-keeper in her chosen costume, he adapted the proper "besotted suitor" pose. Arms hanging low, fingers linked, and legs slightly spread. Perfect timing. The primary bedroom door opened, and Jane glided to the staircase, Rolex at her side.

Punch, punch, punch. Conrad took one internal blow after the other. She wore a black gown with puffed sleeves and a corset that cinched to her curves. A lacy, bustled skirt flared at her waist, the hem pooling on the floor. Pinned to the side of her head was a shiny top hat with a swath of netting that covered a portion of her face. Her bangs hung free, but she'd slicked back the rest, anchoring the dark locks in a tight bun.

A Victorian lady by day and an enchanting gravekeeper by night. Conrad could not look away.

She blushed as she met his gaze and descended the stairs. Rolex remained up top, clearly plotting Conrad's demise.

Conrad winked at him before extending his arm to Jane. A smile bloomed as she accepted.

"There are no words good enough to describe you," he told her.

"Trust me, your eyes are saying plenty." Flirty and charming, she gave him a once-over. Did she realize she licked her lips before giving him a stern frown? "And you. Very agent-y."

"I hate this, by the way," Beau interjected, swiping up a lantern he'd set aside earlier. All kinds of grumpiness layered his tone. "In case anyone was wondering."

Jane patted the vet's cheek as Conrad led her past him. "You're welcome. You look fantastic."

They made their way outside and navigated a lantern-lit cobblestone path to the newly erected dais. Beau took a place at Jane's left while Conrad flanked her right. Wasn't long before the first guests arrived.

He texted Fiona: *Event about to start.*

"Hello and welcome to a night sure to haunt your memories for eternity," Jane called, smiling and waving.

"Before I forget," Beau said, wrestling a small keypad from his tiny pocket. He handed it to Jane, who stuffed it in a pocket of her own. "Press the button when you want more light."

As other guests poured in from the parking lot, Conrad examined the growing sea of faces. The clerk from the hardware store. The barista from the coffee shop. He spotted Abigail Waynes-Kirkland with two men he hadn't met. Yet. More people attended than he'd predicted, some even spilling into the Reflection Center to mill about the stone benches. Still, he'd prepared for this too.

A message came in.

Barrow: The widow is here.

The other agent had arrived an hour ago, and now monitored the camera feed along with the sheriff and a few of his deputies.

Beau set the lantern near Jane's feet with an irritated huff. "People are staring at me."

"Not you," Jane muttered. Without looking at Conrad, she managed to focus on him. "Did you have to bring the badge?" she whispered. "And the gun on your hip? Seriously Conrad."

Yes. Seriously. "All the better to protect you with."

She glanced at him over her shoulder. "You've got to dial down your level of menace, at least."

Why? "I want everyone to know I'm here, and I'm watching." He exaggerated a scowl, earning a sigh from her.

"I hate this," Beau muttered.

"So you've said." Exasperation layered Jane's voice. "Six times."

"Have I mentioned how much *I* like your new look?" Conrad asked the other man, doing his best to deadpan.

Beau crossed his arms. "Shut it. I make bad look good."

"I have the same garments in different colors," Jane told Conrad. "If you'd prefer to be co-groundskeeper for the night, I'll grab them."

Not for ten million dollars and a get out of jail free card with Rolex. "Hard pass."

Mrs. Hotchkins joined the crowd, walking into his line of sight. He studied her. The woman reminded him of a wounded bird. Embarrassed, betrayed, and helpless, yet still grief-stricken over the man who'd caused her heartache.

"See?" Jane squealed, noticing the widow. "It's working. I just got my first big break. I'm now relatively certain there's someone in town who *didn't* do the crime."

She'd acquitted Tiffany Hotchkins? Why? Because of the widow's sadness?

Did anyone have a heart as soft as Jane's?

Movement in the crowd drew his notice. People parted like the Red Sea, allowing Abigail Waynes-Kirkland to beeline toward the widow. The two women embraced and linked arms in solidarity.

Conrad's phone vibrated again.

> Barrow: Caroline Whittington is parking. Dr. Garcia and his family just pulled into the lot. Emma Miller and her ex aren't far behind.

Was a killer soon to enter their midst? Or were they already mingling with the guests?

Tensing, Conrad leaned down to put his lips directly over Jane's ear. "This is still a terrible idea."

Far from convinced, she smirked without even glancing at him. "You'll change your tune when I solve the entire case later tonight."

"Oh, you're resolving everything tonight, are you?" *Do not smile. Do not!*

"Yes, sir. I am." To the crowd, she grinned and waved. "Hello and welcome to a night sure to haunt your memories for eternity."

Whittington joined the throng, easy to spot in a bright yellow jacket. Hmm. A jacket. In the summer heat. Why? Unlike him, she wasn't carrying a concealed weapon. Was she?

As soon as the Garcias reached the area, the physician assistant sidled toward them.

Mrs. Miller wasn't far behind with Mr. Miller at her side. Were they trying to present a picture of solidarity? Too bad; they were failing. Both sported terse faces, their movements awkward.

The nurse wore all black and gloves. Gloves. Planning to touch something she shouldn't?

He texted Fiona: *Even closer to the kick off.*

155

The noise level grew in volume, and Conrad caught snippets of whispered conversations. Jane's name came up multiple times. His name too. Speculating on the special agent's relationship with the "cemetery girl?" He was unbothered by their conjecture—until he noticed Jane's rising upset. Her breathing quickened, the color draining from her cheeks. Tension breached her air of calm, the greatest crime of all. He almost swooped her into his arms and carried her away.

What had caused this kind of fear?

Needing to do something, he stepped into her personal space and gathered her close, acting as an anchor. "Jane. Focus on me. Breathe in. Out. Good. Did I tell you how beautiful you look in that dress? The hat is...not terrible."

His attempt at humor did the trick, and she laughed softly.

Much better. "Calm now?" he asked, relieved but still confused.

Determined, she nodded and lifted her chin as a clock tower gonged in the distance. Midnight.

Tour time.

Ignore the dropping sensation in your stomach. For her sake.

Jane raised her chin another notch. "All right boys, it's showtime."

CHAPTER FOURTEEN

Protect what you love. If you don't, you have no one but
yourself to blame when you lose it.
–A Gravekeeper's Guide to Dating

*C*onrad braced for what came next.

As graceful as a ballerina, Jane lifted the lantern
and glided to the edge of the dais. "Welcome, foolish
mortals," she called, then exaggerated a wince. "I mean, brave
souls. I suggest you gird your loins, for you are soon to meet
the spirits that haunt this cemetery, and there's no turning
back." With her free hand, she reached into her pocket to
clasp the keypad Beau had given her. Evidenced by the
sudden flood of light all around. Right on cue, as if she'd
collaborated with nature, a burst of wind blustered through
the trees, rustling the limbs.

When sounds of distress rose from the masses, she practically preened. She'd hit her groove, and he loved every
second of it.

"Are you ready to enter into the land of the dead?" She

thrust the lantern at Conrad without glancing his way, expecting him to act.

He fought a grin—a common occurrence in her presence.

And she wasn't done. She held out her hands, encouraging both him and Beau to aid her descent from the dais. But they didn't move fast enough for her liking. From the side of her mouth, she whispered fiercely, "Help me!"

The smile cracked free as he and Beau hopped to, rushing to obey.

"I'll follow the group from the rear," the vet explained, jogging off.

Conrad corralled his amusement and returned the lantern to its rightful owner, saying, "I'll remain at your side at all times. Don't even think about ditching me."

"Do you hear me complaining?" she asked, seeming to forget him only a second later. All confidence and expectation, she swept forward, purring to the crowd, "Follow me. If you dare."

Paper lanterns provided illumination as she led the attendees along a cobblestone path, sharing tidbits of information about the different gravesites. True to his word, he remained at her side.

"The words *graveyard* and *cemetery* can be used interchangeably, but not churchyard," she explained. "As the name implies, a churchyard is reserved for burials that adjoin a church."

Though he wanted to enjoy every nuance of her expression and each dramatic gesture she performed, he kept his focus on the people closest to them. While some paid her polite attention, most conveyed obvious hope for more than a history lesson. Soon, whispers arose and expressions turned sour. The more headstones, memorials, and various angel statues they passed, the more a sense of impatience grew.

Jane paused at a gravestone and motioned to a symbol he hadn't noticed when he'd hung the lights. It reminded him of the fleur-de-lys. Small triangles topped three lines that were joined at the base. Had she chosen this site on purpose? Was there a connection to the gold?

"The allure of secret societies is hard to resist," she said, and he knew. Yes, she'd chosen this site on purpose. "You may have heard rumors about the Order of Seven, Aurelian Hills's own secret society with ties to hidden stashes of gold that were buried throughout this town. Are these stories real, or tall tales to tell children to keep them occupied on hot Georgia afternoons? Solve the riddle, find the prize."

Despite the size of the tour group, movement and conversation ceased. Each eye and ear trained on Jane. She'd brought up the subject on everyone's mind.

She rolled on with impressive ease, saying, "As the legend goes, when the gold tapped out, the descendants of our earliest miners resorted to alchemy. They were determined to create their own ore. So, each family became responsible for a single element, and they were given a symbol to go with it. You'll find those patterns etched on different headstones and hidden throughout the oldest parts of Aurelian Hills. The figure on this grave marker represents silver."

The crowd's excitement level sharpened. Whispers rose anew, and restless movements started up again. A need to be the one who solved the riddle and found that prize filled the night air.

Someone in this assembly might kill for said prize.

"The lost gold of Aurelian Hills. Truth or fairy tale?" Jane asked, adding fuel to the fire. "I'll let you decide."

As she continued on with the tour, she lost a good chunk of the crowd. They wandered to the left and the right, spurred into a hunt. There went Whittington. Emma Miller shot off seconds later, and Anthony Miller wasn't far behind.

Oh, and there went Abigail Waynes-Kirkland and Tiffany Hotchkins. Where was Garcia?

Nowhere on the grounds could anyone escape the cameras. No place Barrow and the team couldn't reach in a matter of minutes.

Jane noticed the thinning audience and evinced disappointment. Had the little cupcake hoped the people stayed engaged until the end, more desperate to learn about her beloved Garden of Memories than find gold?

They motored onward, and the crowd thinned further. How much longer did Jane plan to pretend nothing was amiss?

"More and more people are branching off," he pointed out, just to get the ball rolling.

"Thank you, Captain Obvious," she muttered, and yes, she continued on. But the murmurs were increasing.

"Where is it?" someone called. "Show us the gold!"

"Actually," Jane responded with fake cheer, "the Gold family isn't buried here, but if you'll look to your right, you'll notice—"

"I found it!" a woman shouted from the direction of Autumn Grove. "I found where Dr. Hots was murdered!"

That was all it took. A range of emotions pulsed from the remaining guests, many of whom shot off like bullets, quickly vanishing in the darkness.

Jane sighed. "We might as well join them." She didn't wait for his reply but shot off, too.

Conrad shouldered his way forward, reclaiming his spot at her side.

"How dare you!" a woman shouted. He recognized the voice of Mrs. Hotchkins.

Other shouts rang out. As Jane and her dress picked up speed, he matched her pace. Then he spotted the reason for the commotion. The widow stood with her "friend," Ms.

Waynes-Kirkland, who was wagging a finger in Emma Miller's tear-stained face. No sign of Garcia or Whittington.

"Haven't you done enough damage?" the friend demanded. As if she hadn't done the same thing.

The nurse crumpled into herself, as if weighed down by guilt and shame. "I'm sorry. I never meant to hurt you, Tiff. But I loved him, too."

The crowd congregated around the trio, enthralled by the drama and momentarily distracted from their search for gold. Conrad let the verbal confrontation continue. If someone admitted to doing something criminal...

He remained at the ready, however, in case things took a bad turn. Which they did in a blink. Wailing with misery, the widow threw herself at Mrs. Miller. They crashed to the ground and rolled, pulling hair and scratching. Actually, Hotchkins pulled and scratched. Miller accepted the abuse as her due. Or to gain public's support, despite her past actions.

Conrad sighed and rushed over, but Jane darted ahead of him.

"No! Stop this!" she commanded.

He picked up the pace, his longer legs getting him to the combatants faster. He wrenched the battling pair apart.

Beau arrived shortly after, telling him, "Garcia led nowhere" as he assumed responsibility for the widow, who fought him and burst into sobs before crumpling again.

Conrad released Miller, but kept his focus trained on her, his number one suspect. She looked ready to bolt.

Where were Barrow and the deputies? Did they have a more pressing matter elsewhere? Was a guest doing something they shouldn't?

Jane's breath suddenly hitched. "You did it," she snarled, dropping the lantern. Her eyes remained narrowed on Ms. Miller's scab-laden arms. "You're the cat endangerer. That, I know."

The crowd drew closer.

"Jane." Conrad kept his body aimed toward the on-comers, his arms stretched out in the universal *stay back* pose. "Whatever you're thinking, don't." He could imagine the options whizzing through her mind. Citizen's arrest. Shouting match. Command Beau to dig a hole. "Stand down."

She didn't seem to hear him. With a quiet tone, she told Miller, "The only question now is whether or not you're the killer. You were in my house, and you scared my baby. He could have died. He could have died as terribly as Dr. Hotchkins. Because of you."

Conrad knew the second a bomb of fury exploded inside her. Her jaw tightened, and she balled her fists. Then Jane and her dress launched at Miller, and there was no stopping them. Boom! Impact. Once again, two women grappled over the ground. Difference was, Mrs. Miller fought back.

Beau had his hands full with the widow. Stomach in knots, Conrad moved to end the battle between Jane and her foe. From the corner of his eye, however, he tagged Mr. Miller, who barreled through the curious crowd. The attorney had his sights on the gravekeeper as she drew back a fist, intending to give Emma Miller a taste of her fury.

Mr. Miller lunged, sure to intervene. Conrad dove for him, stopping him midway. By the time they hit the ground, he had a firm hold on his target.

He flipped the flailing attorney to his stomach to cuff him and hopefully prevent Jane from landing her blow. Alas. She knocked her opponent out cold. And just like that, the fight was over.

As soon as she realized what she'd done, she grinned and jumped up, demanding, "Someone call Fiona. Tell her what I did. Oh, and maybe round up a visiting doctor. Or two." She shook her hand and winced.

Multiple people cried, "Dr. Garcia!" Some shouted for Whittington.

Conrad cuffed the attorney's hands behind his back. Mr. Miller wasn't under arrest yet, but he had some explaining to do. And Jane? She hadn't acted in self-defense when she attacked the nurse. If Emma Miller pressed charges, he must handcuff and take into custody the woman he planned to date.

"Emma did it," Jane said, adjusting her gown and focusing on Conrad as he helped the attorney into a sitting position. "She's my intruder. She might be the murderer too!"

"Maybe." Probably. So why wasn't he satisfied with the thought? "I'll question her, I promise you."

Caroline Whittington pushed her way through the crowd. "I'm here, I'm here. Who's my patient?"

"Emma," Jane announced, still so proud.

The medical professional got busy checking the nurse's vitals. Hmm. No longer did she wear that bright yellow jacket. So where'd she ditch the coat and why? Without it, one couldn't help but notice the black bodysuit suctioned to her slender frame. Was that a smear of dirt on her throat? Where had she been and what had she been doing?

"Take her to the clinic without jostling her too much," the redhead commanded. "I haven't found any signs of a concussion, but I'd like to do a more thorough examination considering the length of time she's remained unconscious."

Right now, the nurse's well-being outweighed his need to keep his suspects close. And really, he had no legal right insisting either woman remain.

"I'll carry her," Beau said.

A gleam of calculation entered Jane's eyes. She clutched her stomach and exaggerated a wince. "Oh no. Was I injured internally during the fight I just won? I should probably get checked out, too."

Conrad groaned.

Whittington rushed over to check on Jane. After a swift evaluation, she proclaimed, "You'll come, too."

No. No, no, no. Absolutely not. What did his gravekeeper think she'd be able to do, tagging along with two murder suspects? "I'm sure you'll recover. I can't leave until my team arrives." Where were they? They should have shown up already. "You'll stay here with me." Especially if he officially detained her. Which he would absolutely do. Unless there *was* something wrong with her. An inner bleed she knew nothing about. Had Whittington discovered a problem during that thirty second exam?

He scrubbed a hand over his face.

"Allow her to suffer with what is clearly a legitimate ailment?" Beau showed him no mercy, only amusement. He jogged over to gently scoop Emma into his arms. "Don't be so cruel, Conrad. I'll drive Jane to the clinic. Since she isn't under arrest, she's free to go. Isn't she?"

He couldn't legally detain her, and he wanted her checked out ASAP. But he didn't trust Whittington or Miller, who moaned as she woke. On the other hand, he had no concrete proof—yet—of either woman's guilt.

"She is," he admitted reluctantly.

Jane beamed a smile at him, not displaying a hint of pain. He pursed his lips.

"I'll take care of things," the vet said before starting off with Emma. Whittington followed, with Jane close on her heels. Along the way, she glanced back at Conrad.

He maintained eye contact but stayed put. He couldn't leave the scene, not with the attorney bound.

Jane raced back, slamming into him. His heartbeat sped up as he wound an arm around her, holding her close.

She kissed his cheek, batting her lashes at him. "I'll be fine, I promise."

"You better be." Frustration razed his nerves. "I know you consider Emma the killer, and you want to remain by her side. For my peace of mind, stay here."

"Conrad," she rasped, flattening her palm to his chest, "you don't ask a star to stop shining. You make a wish and hope for the best. And Emma isn't the only reason I'm going."

How could anyone argue with a woman like this? How? "When this is over, I'm placing you under immediate house arrest. Just see if I don't. I'll be your jailer."

A toothy smile appeared. "Maybe."

"Jane," Beau called in the distance, and she gasped, as if remembering another world existed beyond them.

Maybe Conrad did the same.

"I've got to run," she said as he tensed, not ready to let her go. Hesitating, she chewed on her bottom lip. "Listen. Don't be mad, but I think Caroline is guilty of something major. Maybe murder, who knows? But don't worry. I'm gonna get answers. Okay, see ya. Bye!" Off she went, leaving Conrad sputtering.

Had he just made a huge mistake, letting his cupcake leave with two women suspected of committing violence? Sweat broke out along his nape. Was she right? And why, why, why did she insist on putting herself in harm's way? *Must get to that clinic as quickly as possible.*

Finally, agents and deputies arrived on the scene. Conrad might have trouble corralling Jane, but he had no problem taking control of the situation and spitting out orders. To Hightower, he barked, "Pick two agents and head to Hotchkins's clinic. Keep your eyes on Whittington, Miller and Ladling at all times." To another agent. "Take Mr. Miller's statement and let him go." Another agent. "Calm Tiffany Hotchkins." Deputies. "Escort the guests to the parking lot. No one leaves without making a statement."

A flurry of activity erupted. "Where's Barrow?" he demanded.

"Still in front of the screens," a random agent replied.

Conrad hurried to the old business center near the back of the property. His partner had cleared the accumulated knickknacks in the foyer where he'd set up. He'd also dusted. The air smelled of pine cleaner.

"Tell me," Conrad commanded as he joined Barrow at a makeshift desk laden with equipment.

"Emma Miller accidentally on purpose put herself in front of Tiffany Hotchkins a dozen times, actively attempting to be noticed by someone who was obviously in a daze. Anthony Miller chased after Caroline Whittington, who navigated the cemetery like a pro. I made a judgment call and sent a couple agents after them. She was clearly searching for something. The lawyer lost her once, but hung back as soon as he found her. When the shouts erupted, both headed your direction in a hurry."

What had everyone searched for? "Why are you still here? What are you looking for?"

"Gold. Jewelry. Something to prove Ms. Whittington has been here before."

"Show me the feed," he intoned.

CHAPTER FIFTEEN

*A dry sense of humor will take you far. Maybe even deep
into a gravekeeper's heart. I said MAYBE.
—A Gravekeeper's Guide to Dating*

*B*arrow punched in a few commands on a laptop
and four different panes appeared on the screen, a
separate part of the cemetery highlighted in each. He fast-
forwarded to the point Caroline Whittington broke from the
crowd and discarded her yellow jacket behind a cluster of
bushes. No doubt she'd hoped to hide her activities in the
darkness.

As she moved, she sped from one pane to another.
Anthony Miller followed her, as expected, but did nothing
else. Intending to catch her in the midst of an illicit act? She
used her cell phone as a flashlight, hastily scanning the
cobblestone paths, flowerbeds, and dirt. A few times, she
paused to pick up and discard a small rock.

"Whatever she's searching for is no bigger than a penny, is
my guess" Barrow observed.

Conrad experienced an explosion of clarity. She was the

killer. He knew it. Felt it. All the little things added up. An arrival to town shortly after the museum debuted its exhibit. Being called hon. The gold hunting partner known as honey-bun. The fleur-de-lys symbol, and her dismissal of the gold rumors. Offering a multitude of other suspects, even at the risk of spotlighting herself. Adding Jane's name to the list of possible lovers to complicate matters. Whittington hadn't checked out a treasure hunting book from the library as Mrs. Miller and Mrs. Waynes-Kirkland had done, but why would she need to? A seasoned treasure hunter kept a collection at home.

Maybe she'd done it to fund her cancer research. If she researched. Maybe she craved the hunt.

On the screen, Whittington jumped and spun in Mr. Miller's direction. Detected him at last? The moment she heard the ruckus caused by fighting guests, she jerked into action, racing back to Autumn Grove, accidentally leaving her jacket behind.

"That's it," Barrow said. "Want to see it again?"

"No need." A scenario played through Conrad's head. Whittington and Hotchkins bonded over their mutual love of treasure hunting. They joined forces and romantic feelings developed. Because Hotchkins. Then she discovered his exam room brothel. When he dug up Rhonda Burgundy's grave and found a nugget, she snapped. In a fit of rage, she hit him with a crowbar. After watching him die, realization set in. She could go to prison for the rest of her life.

Before the installation of cameras, the couple must have cased the cemetery on multiple occasions, learning the direction of various paths, noting when Jane closed the gate and went to bed. Conrad ground his molars at the thought of her unwitting vulnerability. Time of death was just after one, and Jane hadn't started morning rounds until sunup. That had given Whittington several hours to clean up any evidence and wipe away footprints. In the process, she lost the gold nugget. Like any treasure hunter worth her salt, she'd wanted it back, no matter the risk.

"It's Whittington. I'm confident," he told Barrow. "Jane is with her." He didn't stick around to debate the finer points of his conclusion, just ran for his car and jumped behind the wheel.

Lights flashing, he sped along the roads. Luckily most of the town's residents still congregated at the Garden, freeing up the streets. He radioed Hightower, who led the team keeping watch over Jane, Whittington, and Miller. "Stay ready." *Jane is with Beau. She'll be okay.* "At the first hint of trouble, sweep in. I have reason to believe Caroline Whittington killed Hotchkins."

"We're in the parking lot," Hightower said. "The group is inside, and the medical center is locked."

A safety precaution, or sinister preplanning? "Break the lock," he instructed. "Do whatever you need to do."

"Yes, sir."

Conrad arrived minutes later, just as an agent kicked in the door. Wood and debris flew as the entrance gave way. He palmed a weapon and went in directly behind Hightower.

No sign of anyone in the lobby. Or the hall. Twelve closed exam rooms. The other agents swept the corridor, entering one space after another in perfect precision, just as they'd learned at the academy. Slow and steady. Too slow.

Screw that. Conrad shouted, "Jane!"

Metal clanged ahead. There. He rushed forward and burst into a room, aiming his weapon and scanning the area. Beau lay on the floor, out cold. Jane perched at an odd angle on the exam table, her body seemingly boneless. Drugged? Whittington held a pair of scissors to her throat, using her patient as a threat.

His every muscle tensed. Fear flooded him. The other agents rushed in, flanking his sides.

Conrad needed to help her. To do that, he must first calm. Deep breath in. Out. Focus. He went cold and steady. "Let her go," he commanded the other woman. "Hurting her will only make things worse for you."

Whittington released a series of desperate, shallow breaths. "I'm leaving with her. I'll drop her off somewhere once I'm safe."

Only if he were dead. "No, ma'am, you are not leaving here with her. There is no scenario where I allow you to harm her and escape, either. Letting her go is your best chance of having a future."

Jane's fingers twitched, and she gasped. "Conrad."

There was no stopping his gaze as it zoomed to hers.

She beamed a radiant smile at him, so confident in her ability to overcome. "I've got this. Trust me."

"Be quiet and let me think," Whittington demanded, tension surrounding her like a shield. She may be a killer, but it didn't come naturally to her.

In a shocking rush of movement, Jane threw back her head, slamming her skull into the PA's nose. Blood spurted— another bull's eye. The gravekeeper expertly executed a move he'd taught her, clasping her attacker's wrist and pushing.

Whittington wheeled backward, releasing the weapon. Conrad wasted no time, hurrying over to immobilize the offender and arrest her. Beau lay mere inches away, glaring and gritting his teeth as he fought to mobilize.

"Radio for an ambulance," Conrad told an agent as Hightower read Whittington her rights. He checked the vet's pulse. Strong. Excellent.

The agent finished the radio exchange. "They'll be here in less than five."

Good. Very good. He straightened and turned, tenderly

cupping Jane's cheeks. The sweetest relief rained over him. She was alive and well, and nothing else mattered. "You and Beau will be checked out without argument. Once you're cleared, go home. I'll wrap up and drive to you. Tonight we talk."

"Yes, please," she said, melting against him.

They went silent as they clung to each other. No words were necessary at this time.

When the paramedics arrived, they transported Jane and Beau in one ambulance and Whittington and Conrad in another. Though he didn't see Jane again, he spoke with the agents who took her statement and learned Whittington injected her with a neuromuscular inhibitor. The kind used in general anesthesia. No lasting side effects. Jane got a gold star bill of health, and his knees almost buckled with the force of his relief.

He also checked on Beau and his ultra-short shorts, who got their own gold stars.

When Conrad was able, he texted updates to Fiona. Mostly complaints about Jane's expert ability to reach the danger zone, whatever the situation. Her replies helped keep him sane.

Fiona: What do you mean the doctors won't tell you about Jane, despite your badge? Marry her right there in her hospital room, and they've got to tell you everything!

Fiona: Yes, she lacks personal safety awareness but who doesn't? I seem to recall you agreeing to participate in tonight's shenanigans. Speaking of, now that the case is basically closed and you're obviously pursuing Jane hard core, shall I set you a plate at the table tonight? I'm making those pancakes I promised you.

> Fiona: Might I give you a bit of advice? Since I'm certain you just said yes, here it is— when she cuts you from her life, and she will, don't get offended. She's fighting fear, not you.

He needed to hear more about this curse.

He texted back: *Jane says she's a victim of the Ladling curse. Care to elaborate?*

> Fiona: If she hasn't told you then it's not my place to say.

Conrad figured as much.

Upon Whittington's medical discharge, he escorted her to the GBH offices, where he oversaw a tearful confession.

"Have you ever loved someone so much you'd do anything to make them happy?" she asked with a sniffle, a protesting lawyer beside her. A woman she ignored. "I never meant to hurt him."

Her attorney heaved a heavy sigh. "Ms. Whittington, once again I must advise–"

"He ruined *everything*," the physician assistant said, talking over her council. The desire to finally explain her side of the story must be too strong to resist. "He made me feel like the only person alive. *I'm* the one he planned to leave his wife to be with. Me. But all the while he was cheating on me." Bitter laugh. "And yes, I recognize the irony. The cheater cheated. I could have forgiven him for the infidelity. The others were a means to an end. They meant nothing to him. But I couldn't forgive his attempt to steal my gold." Rage sparked in her watery eyes. "I came to this awful town after reading an article about the museum's exhibit. I did the research and grunt work, and some playboy doctor thinks he can keep my reward?"

So much for cancer research. "Are you saying you killed him after he found gold?" Conrad asked, offering her a tissue.

She accepted and dabbed at her face. "Yes, but only because he deserved it. He was so smug. Thought there was nothing I could do to stop him. Well, I showed him there was plenty I could do."

The attorney shook her head. "Just tie the whole case up in a bow for him," she muttered.

"I hit him, and he fell," Whittington said, powering on. "I tried to clean up the mess as best as I could."

"You lost the nugget in the process."

She gave a jerky nod. "It's mine. No matter where I am, it's mine. If Jane or anyone else finds it, I want it back. *I* pieced together the steps taken by the Order of Seven. Me. Not him. Me."

"I'm sure something could be arraigned," Conrad said. Or not. "Tell me how you pieced things together." So he could stop anyone else from doing the same.

Arching a brow at him, she asked, "Thinking about finding your own treasure, agent? Too bad. You'll get no help from me."

"I'll try to recover," he replied drily. "Did you paint the cult symbol on the cars?"

"Yes. Marcus didn't do as promised and keep his big mouth shut about the gold. He told his wife, among others. I feared he'd mentioned my name but figured I would come up at some point either way. As a lover or a collaborator. Or both. I hoped to make myself look as innocent as possible in the meantime. Who spray paints her own car?"

Made sense in a warped way. Still, a final question remained. "Why break into Jane's home?" He poured her a glass of water. Might as well be a good host while grilling her for information.

She sipped and breathed deep. "I didn't. I ensured Emma

found enough evidence to suggest Marcus had stashed secret photos and videos of their affair at the cemetery, intending to blackmail her. I'd noticed your interest in her and hoped she would incriminate herself."

Maybe Mr. and Mrs. Miller attended tonight's event together hoping to snatch the supposed photos and videos of Emma with Hotchkins. But why follow Whittington? Unless they'd suspected her of lying?

Once the PA wrote and signed her confession, Conrad left the interrogation room to meet Barrow in his office. Pictures of the guy's kids and finger-painted drawings covered the walls. The agent had earned the same certifications Conrad had, but those were nowhere to be seen. He'd never noticed the difference before. Now that he had, he thought he might want to make a few changes in his own workspace. There was a certain smiling face he wouldn't mind glimpsing on his wall every day.

"How did the interview with Emma Miller go?" Conrad asked, sinking into a chair in front of his partner's desk.

Barrow rolled away from his computer screen. "Unlike your witness, she listened to her attorney. Not her husband or Hagger, by the way."

"You implying your interrogation was more difficult than mine?"

"I thought I outright stated it." The other man smiled. "Why don't you ask me the question you really want to ask."

Very well. "Is Mrs. Miller pressing charges against Jane?"

"Mrs. Miller isn't. As long as Ms. Ladling doesn't."

"Deal." Conrad was certain Jane would agree. He planned to ask when he reached the cottage. If he survived the drive to her house, of course. At the moment, he felt as though he might burst out of his skin. He needed to get his eyes on her. Hug her. Ensure her safety and well-being. Then talk. *Then* kiss her and never stop.

He stood and headed for the exit, only to pause at the door. "And thank you, Barrow. I appreciate your help." The nurse's offer had probably come after some gentle prodding.

The agent leaned back in his chair and seemed to study Conrad with a mental magnifying glass. Satisfied with what he deduced, he nodded. "Good for you. She's, um, quite the character."

"Yes, she is." Conrad was grinning as he trekked to his car.

Once he'd buckled in, he texted Fiona: *Set out that extra plate. I'm on my way.*

He all but vibrated with anticipation the entire trip to Jane's front door. Finally, he was rasping his knuckles against the wood. As he waited, he braced against the frame. His ears twitched, different sounds registering. Thumping footsteps. Squeaking hinges. Suddenly she stood before him, the most wholesome, welcome sight in existence. Jane, wearing a fitted white tee, flowing pajama pants covered with Rolex's face and fluffy slippers with cat heads. Punch.

Eyes wide and soft, she said, "Hello, Conrad."

"Hello, sweetheart." He smiled, everything right in his world. "Are you ready for our talk?"

She flashed him a return smile so stunning he forgot the things he'd planned to say. All the things blocking a possible relationship. Her cat. Conrad's habit of protecting his heart. How she enjoyed inserting herself into every part of a murder investigation. At least that problem had solved itself. It wasn't like Aurelian Hills was a hotbed of crime.

"What happened to immediate house arrest?" she asked with a smooth as silk voice that did things to him. "I've been looking forward to wearing your cuffs."

The moment her words registered, he chuckled. Did she have any idea what she'd—

"I meant...I...you," she sputtered. Oh, yeah. She'd figured it out. "I demand a trial first!"

"Excellent. I'll grill you with questions." The relationship talk of his dreams.

Except, panic flashed over her expression. "Um. I don't know. Maybe we shouldn't..." She darted her gaze in different directions. *Oh no.* The raisins were rising to the surface, no doubt about it. "I don't think we should speak ever again," she said, and he sighed. Yeah. Definitely the raisins.

Conrad intended to take Fiona's advice and roll with the punches. Starting something with Jane Ladling was worth any trouble she tossed his way. He stepped forward, entering the house, forcing her to walk backward. "I'm starved, sweetheart. Let's do our not speaking over blueberry pancakes."

He walked around her then, leaving her gaping.

WANT MORE? You can find Gena Showalter and Jill Monroe hanging out together on their Patreon.

BOOKS in the Jane Ladling Series
   Romancing the Gravestone
   No Gravestone Left Unturned
   Game of Gravestones
   Twelve Graves of Christmas
   Conrad: Falling For the Gravekeeper

BOOKS in the Writing Fiction Series:
All Write Already
All Write Already Workbook
The Write Life
Write Now! An All Write Already Journal

ABOUT GENA SHOWALTER

Gena Showalter is the New York Times and USA TODAY bestselling author of multiple "unputdownable" series in paranormal, contemporary, and young adult romance.

Learn more about Gena, her menagerie of rescue dogs, and all her upcoming books at genashowalter.com

ALSO BY GENA SHOWALTER

Immortal Enemies

Start with: Heartless

.

Rise of the Warlords

Start with: The Warlord

.

Lords of the Underworld

Start with: The Darkest Night

.

White Rabbit Chronicles

Start with: Alice in Zombieland

.

Tales of an Extraordinary Girl

Start with: Playing with Fire

.

Everlife

Start with: Firstlife

.

Original Heartbreakers

Start with: The Secret Fling

.

Angels of the Dark:

Start with: Wicked Nights

.

Otherworld Assassins

Start with: Last Kiss Goodnight

·

Gena's Complete List of Releases:

GenaShowalter.com/books

ABOUT JILL MONROE

Jill Monroe is the international best selling author of over fifteen novels and novellas. Her books are available across the globe and **The Wrong Bed: Naked Pursuit** has been adapted for the small screen for Lifetime Movie Network.

When not writing, Jill makes her home in Oklahoma with her husband, enjoys daily walks with her dog Zoey, texting with her two daughters and collecting fabric for items she'll sew poorly.

Learn more about Jill at jillmonroe.com

ALSO BY JILL MONROE

Sworn Series:

Sworn Promises

Sworn Duty

Sworn By A Kiss

Sworn Protector

.

Wrong Bed Series

Naked Thrill

Naked Pursuit*

*(Now a movie from Lifetime Movie Network)

.

From Hallmark:

At The Heart of Christmas

.

Spicy Romance:

Fun & Games

Treasure in the Sand (novella)

.

Jill's Complete List of Releases:

https://jillmonroe.com/allbooks/

Made in United States
North Haven, CT
26 March 2023